NEXT IN LINE FOR LOVE

From Bestselling Lesbian Romance Author

HARPER BLISS

Other Harper Bliss Books

A Lesson in Love
Life in Bits (with T.B. Markinson)
A Swing at Love (with Caroline Bliss)
No Greater Love than Mine
Once Upon a Princess (with Clare Lydon)
In the Distance There Is Light
The Road to You
Seasons of Love
Release the Stars
Once in a Lifetime
At the Water's Edge
The French Kissing Series
High Rise (The Complete Collection)

the Pink Bean Series

More Than Words
Crazy for You
Love Without Limits
No Other Love
Water Under Bridges
This Foreign Affair
Everything Between Us
Beneath the Surface
No Strings Attached

Copyright © 2019 by Harper Bliss
Cover design by Caroline Manchoulas
Published by Ladylit Publishing – a division of Q.P.S. Projects Limited - Hong Kong
ISBN-13 978-988-79124-8-4
All rights reserved. Unauthorised duplication is prohibited.
This is a work of fiction. Any resemblance of characters to actual persons, living or dead, is purely coincidental.
No part of this book may be reproduced in any form or by any electronic or mechanical means, including information storage and retrieval systems, without written permission from the author, except for the use of brief quotations in a book review.

1

ALI

I ALWAYS GET a faint whiff of stale beer when I enter the Lennox Breweries offices, even though the actual brewing doesn't happen in this building. I shake off the imagined scent and head toward the elevator bank. The lobby feels empty—too empty. What was I expecting? A welcoming committee? That would have been nice, actually.

I make my way to the top floor unescorted, briefly wondering if I got the date wrong. But how could I possibly have gotten it wrong? This is the day I start my journey to becoming Chief Executive Officer of one of the country's oldest breweries.

When the elevator opens to the executive floor, I'm greeted by my brother Sebastian—the last person I want to see.

"Hey, Sis," he says. The smile on his face is already annoying me. "Ready for the big league?" I know the question isn't one born from genuine concern. Sebastian's just here to taunt me. We're both in our thirties, yet insulting each other is still what we do most of when we are together.

"What are you doing here?" I ask, taking his bait.

"I'm here for you, of course." He brings a hand to my shoulder, making me believe, just for a split second, that he can be a nice guy if he really wants to be. "On your big day." He flashes me a smile again—it's only a fraction less annoying this time. "Someone has to make sure you don't fuck up straight away."

"I'm touched." My voice drips with sarcasm. As we progress toward my father's office suite, a few people look up; some even give me a nod or quick wave.

"You'd think the old man would be in an extraordinary mood today, what with his favorite daughter reporting for duty, but he's just as cranky as ever," Sebastian says. "Trust me. It's good that I'm here."

Our father, Jeffrey Lennox, is the kind of man who can strike the fear of God into you with a single, withering look. A man who has gotten used to taking exactly what he wants. And now I'm here to take over his biggest prize.

"If you say so." We approach the glass box that makes up my father's office. He's standing by the window, gazing out over the Los Angeles skyline.

Sebastian looks at his watch. "I do have a meeting that can't be pushed back—not even for *your* arrival, Ali." He gives a curt, ridiculous bow. "You're on your own." So much for my brother being there for me on my big day.

You'd think it wasn't my own father I'm about to greet, what with the way my heart is stomping in my chest. This is ridiculous. And all Sebastian has done is make me more nervous, which was probably his intention.

"Hey, Ali. Right on time." A voice comes from behind me. "Shall we go in?"

"Jill." I nod at the woman who has been Lennox Breweries' Chief Operating Officer for as long as I can remember, although there must have been a time when it wasn't her. My father makes the decisions, Jill Gold implements them.

Unlike the rest of the SoCal population, Jill's not the sort of woman to greet you with a hug. She raps her knuckles against the glass door, opens it, and ushers me into my father's office.

"Alexandra." My father turns to me and opens his arms wide —as though I've just flown in from somewhere far away, instead of seeing him at the house two days ago. Maybe's he's putting on a show for Jill, but why would he? If not for Jill, then for me, perhaps? Where's the crankiness Sebastian was talking about?

"Hi, Dad." I walk toward him but not too close.

He keeps his arms spread, but it's more a showy gesture than any actual desire to give me a proper hug.

"The day has finally come. You've come to take the crown," he says.

"Hardly." I can just about keep from rolling my eyes. "I still need to get my training wheels on."

"Yes, well." He heads behind his large desk. "You know what I mean." He waves for Jill to come closer.

"It makes sense to take you under my wing, Ali," Jill says. "I know everything that happens at this company. Stick with me for a while, and you'll be ready in no time."

"She'll be *your* boss in no time," my father says, his voice gruff.

Jill shrugs off his comment as though she won't mind working for someone much younger than herself—as though she never considered herself for the part of CEO. But she's not a Lennox. It was always going to be either me or Sebastian.

"The first thing we need to do," Jill says, "is make you a viable proposition for the board." She gives a quick shake of the head. "They'll be expecting Sebastian."

"That's what you get when the board's mostly made up of old men," I say. If I'm going to be CEO, I shouldn't mince my words.

"Very true," Jill says before my father can make a comment.

"I haven't exactly been sitting on my ass the past ten years," I say. "You can order Lennox beer in more than a hundred countries around the world these days."

While this is true—I've been working in the family business for a decade now—even I expected Sebastian to be the one to follow in Dad's footsteps, despite him being an entitled, obnoxious douchebag.

But times have changed and suddenly share prices can plummet, even when the most logical successor is announced. When they present me as the next CEO instead of my brother, the share price should stay pretty steady. At least, that's what my father told me when he gauged my interest in the position. It was a heart-warming way to sell me on the whole premise.

"Once we've got the board... on board," Jill says, not a hint of a smile on her face, "we'll take it from there. But that's the first objective. We need to create the idea of stable leadership. Someone who won't rock the boat, but is fresh at the same time."

"No pressure." I glance at Jill. Even though we're in Southern California, she's wearing a black turtleneck sweater.

"Don't worry, Ali. I've got your back." There's something sincere—and therefore very unusual—about her, so I believe her when she says it, although I can't completely shake off the skepticism I was raised with.

The least I can do is give her a warm smile in response.

A knock comes on the door. It's Evelyn, my father's personal assistant. "Dr. Barnes is here," she says.

My father rolls his eyes and sinks into his leather chair.

"Just follow Jill around." He as good as waves us out of the door.

Jill holds the door open for me. I'm at least five inches taller than her.

"I managed to convince him to have his blood pressure

monitored twice a day. He doesn't like it, as you can imagine," she whispers, "but needs must."

I follow her to her office. She points to the wall behind her desk. "We've set you up next door, close to all the action."

"Thanks." I glance around. Jill's office is a smaller replica of my father's. Perhaps mine will be exactly the same as well, but a little smaller still, to represent the current pecking order.

"How is he really doing? In the day-to-day?"

"He's an old man." Jill says it very matter-of-factly. It's good to know she doesn't mince her words either. "He should have stepped down years ago, but he's more stubborn than he's old, so..."

"Tell me about it," I say as though I know all about it. I've only been back in L.A. a few weeks.

"I have some calls to make." Jill looks at her watch. "But how about lunch together?"

"Oh, uh." I slant my head. "I already have plans for lunch."

"With Sebastian?" she inquires. "He can tag along." She grins at me. "If he must."

"Um, no. With my friend Madison. I didn't think today was going to be, like, a whole thing."

"*A whole thing*?" Jill creases her features into an expression I can only interpret as extreme disapproval. "Why do I get the impression you're not taking this very seriously? You're going to be CEO of Lennox Breweries, Ali. This 'whole thing' is going to take up a lot of your time, if not all of it. I hope you're aware of that."

"I'm well aware. It's just that today's the first day. I have the rest of my life to be serious about it." I reach for my cellphone in the side pocket of my blazer. "But if it's so important, I'll have lunch with you instead."

Jill's phone starts ringing. She shoots me one last glance—is that some mild disdain I detect?—and turns to pick it up.

I slink out of her office, in search of my own. Maybe it's

good that we'll have lunch, so I can manage Jill's expectations of me. We already seem to have different ideas of what it means to become the big boss.

2

JILL

"I HOPE we didn't get off on the wrong foot earlier." I'm not sure why I'm being so nice to Ali—probably because she's the boss's daughter. And it's my job to train her to become my next boss.

The sushi I ordered sits untouched between us on the conference table in my office.

"I'm the one who should apologize." Ali doesn't really sound as though she means it. For someone who has been out of the state—and out of the country—for so long, she sounds like a quintessential spoiled brat from Beverly Hills, irritating inflections in her voice included. "Tell me honestly, Jill. Am I nothing more than a figurehead here? Because that's what I've been led to believe. Both by my brother *and* my father. They need me for the optics and that's about it." She glares at the food on the table, making no move to actually eat any of it. Maybe it's not up to her standards.

I've been dealing with Jeffrey Lennox's children since I started my career at Lennox Breweries—although I haven't seen Ali in a very long time. I've often lamented that if Jeffrey wanted his children to succeed him, he should have raised them a little differently, but he was always too busy building his business to put much thought into his offspring.

"Lennox needs you. *All* of you," I say, with feeling. "Not just your pretty face, Ali." I want her to have a chance. She might have spent the past decade living the high life in various European and Asian cities, pretending to be export manager for the company, but if I have my way, Alexandra Lennox will become the next CEO of this company. I'd much rather have her at the helm than her brother, whose privilege has only been increased by the fact he was born male.

"That's the first I've heard of that."

"Look." I open a bottle of overpriced Fiji water. "We have a chance here to usher this company into a new era. The only reason we even have this opportunity is because your brother screwed up one time too many. Because he thinks he can get away with anything. Well, he can't anymore. This is a golden opportunity for us, for you and me, Ali. We can run this company together, if we want."

I hope I've read Ali correctly and that she dislikes her brother as much as I do. I've never seen any evidence to the contrary, but years abroad can change a person.

"And let Sebastian know he cannot run things behind the scenes?" Her face lights up.

"Exactly."

"Maybe we can even push him out in the process," Ali says. "Shouldn't he be in jail or something, anyway?"

"He went to rehab." Lennoxes don't go to jail, I add in my head.

"Fat load of good that did him." She wrinkles up her nose. "Pity there are no rehabilitation centers for first-class douchebags..."

"I take it there have been no grand reconciliations since you've returned?"

Ali's very different from her brother. I can actually have a conversation with her where things are articulated instead of insinuated. I can get to know a few things through her.

"Sebastian wants to drink my blood." Ali leans back in her chair and crosses her arms over her chest. "He won't come out and say it, but he absolutely loathes that Dad has chosen me over him. Even though it's his own stupid fault."

"It's not something he'll get over any time soon. You'll need to watch your back."

"I thought you had my back." Ali draws her lips into a smile.

"I do." I pluck a piece of salmon sashimi from the plate in front of me. "Do you have mine?" The slice of salmon hovers in front of my mouth as I wait for Ali to reply.

"Are we forging some kind of sisterly pact over sushi?"

"We can." I chuckle to make light of it, but it's exactly what I want. If I can get Ali accepted by the board, I can have virtual control of this company once Jeffrey steps down. Our first move, after Senior is out of the door, will be to get rid of Sebastian. All I need is Ali Lennox on my side.

"Okay." Ali doesn't dismiss the idea. "I've always liked you, Jill. You've obviously steered this company through some rough patches, but… I'm not as young and naive as I used to be. And I don't really know you. So I guess your other very important and urgent job is to make me trust you."

"Of course." Perhaps I underestimated Ali a little. I had my guy do some research on her, because I haven't seen much of her while she was gallivanting around the globe. From what I've heard, she likes to party just as much as her brother does, but the substances she uses are always legal, which already makes her a fair bit smarter than Sebastian. "Challenge accepted." I have quite a few years on Ali, and a whole lot more experience in business in general, and this company specifically. Getting her to trust me shouldn't be too hard—as long as I don't make the mistake of underestimating her. She's still a Lennox. After their mother died, Jeffrey might have allowed

Alexandra and Sebastian to do anything they wanted while he escaped into work, but they were both born with Lennox smarts. It runs in their blood.

Ali nods at me sternly, as if I'm her subordinate already.

"Now tell me, how have you been, Ali?" It's time to lighten the mood, and to get to know her all over again. The last time I saw Jeffrey's daughter was at her twin sister's funeral ten years ago.

"Singapore was a hoot," she says. "I wouldn't have minded staying longer. They just really *get* extravagance there. Having a shit ton of money is, like, so normal in some countries."

She sounds a lot like Sebastian right now. They are siblings, after all. But I decide to focus on the other parts of her—and to unearth at least one positive trait I can work with.

"How are *you*?" she asks, much against my expectations. Sebastian never deigns to ask me how I am. No one on this floor does. "Are you married with a couple of brats?" She squints. "Don't tell me you're a grandma already. I won't believe you."

I chuckle. She couldn't be further from the truth. There's a reason why nobody here asks me how I'm doing. I've taught everyone that it's a pointless question. I don't discuss my private life at work, mostly because I don't have one.

"None of that. I've always been married to the job, which I know is a terrible cliché."

Ali examines my face, then nods as though she has suddenly understood something about me. I'm not sure why my palms suddenly feel moist.

"Your dedication to my family's brews is touching," Ali says with a grin on her face. Then she finally picks up a pair of chopsticks and starts to eat.

3

ALI

"WHAT ARE YOU DRINKING?" I ask Madison.

The party has clearly been going on for a while. Just as I was leaving, my father called me into his office to explain his ideas for the future of Lennox Breweries in great detail, making me late. As he droned on and on, the way he does much more these days than he used to, I thought about how I had been looking forward to this party all week and how I had promised Madison I'd be there early, and definitely before any other guests arrived.

"A non-alcoholic IPA," she says. "It's all the rage." Madison doesn't seem cross with me for being late. She's her usual relaxed self.

"Can I see?" She gives me the bottle. "This isn't a Lennox beer," I quickly conclude.

"Lennox doesn't do non-alcoholic IPAs. I'd be surprised if you produced *any* IPAs at all," Madison says. "If you do, they probably taste like dishwater."

"Excuse *moi*." I glare at Madison. We've been poking fun at my family's business all our lives, but now that I actually work there—although not much actual work has been done so far—

it feels somehow inappropriate. "That's *my* company you're talking about."

Madison shrugs. "Now you're back in the motherland, are you still export manager? Can you actually perform your exporting tasks from the great city of Los Angeles? You know, without deserting your best friend for years? If yes, you could have come back to me sooner."

Father as good as made me swear an oath to not tell anyone about the real reason for my return. So far, I've obeyed. It feels weird to not tell Madison, who I've always confided in, even when I lived thousands of miles away. "I think we're trying to figure out a new role for me," I say. It's close enough to the truth so I don't feel like I'm lying to my best friend. I ignore her remark about my physical absence from her life for the past ten years.

I take a sip from her alcohol-free beer. "Not bad."

"Maybe you can be in charge of non-alcoholic beer. Start by introducing it," Madison says.

"Maybe." I don't give the beer back. It has become market research as far as I'm concerned.

We're sitting on the patio overlooking the pool. A few people have stripped down and jumped into the water.

"It feels like I've gone back in time about fifteen years." I glance at Madison. "A pool party."

"Why not? This is L.A. This is what we do." She bumps her knee against mine. "It's hardly been any fun without you, Lennox."

Madison knows why I needed to get away when I did. I can hardly claim I came back a different person, but something inside me has changed. Calmed down, perhaps.

A topless woman jumps into the pool, catching my full attention. When she emerges, her wet hair slicked back, I squint to get a better look at her face. "Is that Angel Ashby?"

"It is," Madison says, and follows up with a chuckle. "You'll never guess who she's dating."

"Wait..." I turn to Madison and study her face. "Not you, right?"

Madison shakes her head. "Do you really think that if I was dating Angel Ashby you wouldn't know about it?"

"I've been away. You might be keeping things from me." I smile at her. "Who?"

"Wendy Nichols."

"*Our* Wendy Nichols?"

"It's allowed these days. At least for B-list actresses. A-list is still quite frowned upon."

"Wow." I take another sip from the alcohol-free beer. It might be all the rage, but I could do with something stronger.

"Look at you all caught up in the gay glitz of Hollywood." I wink at Madison. She recently had a part in *Everything Right Now,* a critically acclaimed but niche Netflix show about a bunch of jaded West Hollywood queers. When I watched it, I joked she was basically playing herself.

"I *am* the queen of gay glitz, darling," she says.

"Oh, really?"

"Well, you were gone so what was I going to do?"

"Take my throne." I glance at her again. "You're very welcome to it."

"So I sit here every weekend, surveying my queendom. It's quite nice." She looks at the people frolicking in her pool.

"You know everyone here, don't you?" I follow Madison's gaze. My eyes are automatically drawn to Angel Ashby. Growing up in L.A. hasn't made me totally immune to Hollywood star power.

"Of course I do. No strangers in my pool."

"She's hot." I know I can say whatever I want in front of Madison.

"Hands off, though. She's with Wendy."

"What do you take me for?"

"I take you for exactly what you are, Alexandra Lennox. A woman who always gets what she wants." I feel Madison's stare on me. "You haven't always considered other people's feelings, Ali. I've seen you put the moves on women who were not available plenty of times before."

"Only because they made themselves available to me," I joke. Although Madison's right. Before I left L.A.—and quite a few years after—I wouldn't have had any qualms hitting on someone like Angel Ashby, even if I knew she was with someone else.

"Obnoxiousness alert," Madison says.

"I was just kidding." I give her a look.

"Do you have a preferred type these days?" she asks. "Butch? Boi? High femme? Low femme? All or any of those?"

"Christ." I turn toward her again. "We do love a good old label in the US of A. I have found that overseas, people are much less boxed in."

"You know, even when you're trying to say something profound, and maybe even potentially correct, you still manage to sound so fucking entitled." Madison chuckles.

"It's part of my charm, Mads." I say it with confidence, but, lately, I have begun to question my privilege somewhat.

"You haven't answered my question," Madison insists.

I gaze around the garden—scanning for prey, as we used to call it. "I quite fancy myself some of that." I discreetly point at a woman reclining in a lounger on the other side of the pool. She has legs for days and is wearing only a skimpy bikini. Her skin glistens from a recent stint in the pool. "Who is she?"

"A girl I know," Madison says enigmatically.

"*Oh.* Does that mean hands-off?" I look her in the eye.

"Nah. It's over."

"You were with her?"

Madison nods. "Just for a little while."

"You stayed friends, obviously."

"Sort of. I didn't really think she'd come tonight and... flaunt her wares like that."

I giggle at how she puts it. "You're not over her? What's her name?"

"Bethany," Madison says wistfully.

"Is there anything I can do to make Bethany like you again?" I bring my face close to hers. "Do you want me to kiss you to make her jealous and realize what she's missing out on?"

"We're not in our crazy twenties anymore." Madison pulls away from me.

"What does that even mean?"

"It means that I don't play games like that anymore. Either someone likes me, or they don't. And if they don't, I'm mature enough to deal with it in an adult way."

"What you're really trying to say," I look into Madison's eyes again, "is that you've gone off kissing me."

She scrunches up her lips. "You were gone a long time. We both had some growing up to do."

"I guess." Nodding, I look over the garden again, at all the women I can't have—well, at least two of them. If I'm being completely honest, it gnaws at me a little. But I try to resist the impulse of, as Madison just put it, taking exactly what I want. I'm trying to actively resist my family's sense of entitlement, which, try as I might to ignore it, is part of the fabric of my being.

4

JILL

"How's the boss's daughter working out?" Linda asks.

She's worked at Lennox as long as I have, and lost her reverence for the people in charge a long time ago. She's also the only one in my department I trust with all my confidential documents.

"The jury's still very much out on that." Ali's only been back a week.

"She's late." Linda taps her watch ostentatiously.

"Only an hour." I know better than to get upset about one of the Lennoxes being late. Although, even in his eighties, Jeffrey's often at the office before I arrive.

"What's the old man thinking, putting someone like that in charge?"

"Ali has potential." I have to believe this. "It's my job to bring that out." I allow myself a small sigh. "You can't really blame her for being who she is. She's never had to take responsibility for anything in her life. She and her brother basically grew up without any formal parenting so..."

"It's a tough job you've got," Linda says. "Trying to transform a trust fund brat into someone capable of running this company."

"You and me both." I smile widely at Linda.

"Leave me out of it, please. I'm very happy working for you, as long as I don't have to deal with the top brass directly. It's not my scene, you know that."

"Ah, and I was going to have her follow you around today."

"It's bad enough that Sebastian walks into my office as though he owns the place at least once a day…"

"Well, technically, he does."

Linda sighs as well now. "Don't you wish for universal basic income sometimes?"

I roll my eyes. "That would barely cover the monthly bill for my parking space."

"You get off on it," Linda says. "It's the only way I can explain you."

"Explain me?" I start pacing. Ali's blatant lateness is beginning to annoy me despite what I said to Linda. "Since when do I need to be explained?"

"You're quite a normal woman, Jill. You shouldn't really fit in with the Lennoxes so well, yet you do. It's always been a bit disconcerting."

I need some time to process Linda's perception of me. "You're basically saying I'm too average to mingle with the one percent?"

"Clearly not." Linda flashes me a big mischievous grin. There's some stumbling in the hallway and then Ali barges into my office.

Linda quickly slips out, giving me a meaningful look as she does.

"Sorry I'm late," Ali says. "Bit of a rough weekend." She pushes her shades higher up her nose. "Madison threw a party on Friday evening and it never really ended." She slumps onto the cracked-leather sofa at the far end of my office.

"Are you hungover?" I ask.

"I wouldn't exactly call it hungover. In fact—" She slaps her palms onto the top of the coffee table. "Did you know that alcohol-free beer is all the rage these days? It's, like, everywhere, Jill."

I suppress a sigh. "It doesn't look like you partook of much of it."

"Well, no, of course I didn't. It gets tiresome after a while and you know how much I adore an expertly mixed cocktail, but—" It's as though Ali only now realizes she's at work. "Anyway, how was your weekend, Jill?" she asks.

"That's none of your business." I stand behind my desk, wishing I was in possession of a more towering presence. I need to find some sort of authority to wield over Ali if this is going to work. I can't let her walk all over me—and turn up hungover on a Monday morning.

"Ouch." Ali slings one long leg over the other. Her hair is pulled into a high ponytail. She's wearing a tailor-made light blue pants-suit that shouldn't really look good on anyone, but it does on her. For all the time I've been around rich people, I've never been able to fathom the secret to them looking so good all the time, as though it takes no effort at all.

"Your father and Sebastian are at the brewery today so at least you haven't incurred their wrath." I sink into my chair. I might as well. When I was first told that Ali would be transferring to head office, I was excited at the opportunity I saw ahead of me. Now, it feels more like I'm babysitting a thirty-something child who's refusing to grow up. But I always knew it would be a challenge—and I'm always up for one of those.

"But I do seem to have incurred the wrath of Jill Gold." Ali slants her head. "How about I take you to brunch to make up for it?"

"How about, instead of playing truant at ten o'clock on a

Monday morning, we put some rules in place. Otherwise, I don't really see how this is going to work out."

"Ah, Jill, you're such a spoilsport. The male Lennoxes are out of the house. I'm the only Lennox left. Let's do something fun. Something female and fun."

Next, she'll propose we take a spa day. I shake my head.

"I'm having a party at my new house this weekend. You should swing by. If we're going to work together in all the ways you propose, we should get to know each other better."

"I don't think so, Ali."

"My dad invites you to his house all the time. Why won't you come to mine? Is it because I don't live in Beverly Hills?"

"I'll think about it, but... believe it or not, some people actually have a job to do. That includes you now."

"Hey." She lowers her shades and glares at me from over the rim. "As far as I'm concerned, I've done my job for today. Hell, for this week. Alcohol-free beer! Let's rake in the cash."

I can no longer hold back my sigh. "It's already in development. We'll be launching it soon. What do you think we do here all day long?"

She hides behind her sunglasses again. "Shit. Who came up with that idea? Please don't tell me it was Sebastian?"

"We have an actual market research department." An idea takes root. "We have many departments in this company."

"Duh," is all she says.

"How about I arrange for you to spend a few weeks at each one?"

"What? Like work experience?"

"Yes, exactly like that."

Ali shakes her head. "Nah. I don't think I'll be a huge fan of that."

"It doesn't matter what you think. I think it's important for you to experience first-hand how each department works."

"Does my father think it's important?"

"He will if I tell him that it is."

She deflates a little. "Let's make a deal," she says. "I'll do my tour of all the departments without complaining, to you or my father, if you come to my party next weekend."

This is what my life has consisted of since I started work at Lennox Breweries: endless negotiations with people like Ali.

"Fine," I say, having no actual intention of going to her house. In my job, I can always come up with a last-minute excuse to get out of something. In fact, over the years, it has become my specialty. "I'll come. But for now, it looks like the market research department really needs you."

5

ALI

I'm not sure how I've found myself in my brother's apartment, but here I am. It's large and starkly decorated with lots of white and black—no room for any grays, it would appear.

"There's a helipad on the roof," he says.

"Of course there is."

"You could have moved into this building." He drops a few ice cubes into a cut-glass tumbler. "I bought the floor below as well."

"As much as I would have adored living underneath you, it wasn't to be."

Sebastian hands me a glass of Scotch on the rocks. Either he has forgotten I don't drink Scotch or he's messing with me. I don't react and just put the glass on the table.

"Your loss." He sips from his drink and then leans back into the white leather sofa.

We sit in silence for a few minutes. I glance at him from the corner of my eye. Sebastian is two years younger than me and sometimes, if I look at him from the right angle, I can still see a shadow of the little Sebastian I remember.

"Why did you invite me here?" I ask when I can no longer bear the silence.

"You're my sister. You lived abroad for ten years. Maybe I feel we should spend some time together." He doesn't look at me when he speaks.

"In contemplative silence?"

"You can speak if you want to." He reaches inside his blazer and produces a small translucent bag with white powder inside.

"Oh, for fuck's sake. You're not going to do your drugs in front of me, Seb. Fuck that. I won't have it."

"What? Now you're not even drinking anymore?" He eyes my untouched glass of Scotch. "You've come back having fully processed all the Lennox traumas and you don't need an easy escape anymore? Because you're going to be CEO and that makes you better than me?"

"What are you even talking about?"

Sebastian throws the little bag onto the table. I'm no expert, but it looks like coke. How very nineties.

"You left. You just fucked off, Ali. To someplace where you didn't have to deal with my or Dad's grief."

He's going straight for the jugular. I have to give him kudos for that.

"It was my right to leave. I had my own grief to deal with."

"Maybe, but you could have come back once in a while. Leah dying aged Dad beyond his years."

"Beyond his years? He's eighty-three. He's old. He was old when she died and he's ten years older now. That's how it goes."

"It's all fucked, anyway. It doesn't matter." He eyes the baggie of coke.

"I'm sorry I couldn't stay. Leah and I..." I stop explaining myself. Seb knows. He's my brother, he *should* know. Then again, there appear to be plenty of things I don't know about him. Like my leaving fucking him up as well. Next he'll tell me I'm responsible for his coke habit.

Because it's all I can think of to do, I reach for the glass of Scotch and pretend to take a sip. The mere scent of it is enough to make me queasy.

"Now you're back, and all Dad can see is you," he says.

"He asked me to return."

"So? That doesn't mean you had to come. Why did you?"

"Because... It was time."

"It's really bad timing for me." He empties his glass and pulls a face as the liquor slides down his throat. "If I'd had another year, a few months even, to get my act together..."

"Dad doesn't have another year. He should take it easy. He looks frail."

"He's Jeffrey fucking Lennox." Sebastian shakes his head. "I always thought he'd live forever."

"Maybe the next generation of Lennoxes will."

"Look." He sits up. "I'm throwing my cards on the table. I know Dad wants to appoint you as his successor because..." He nods at the coke. "Well, you know why. For some reason, I have to be squeaky clean if I want to be the face of LB and I had the bad luck of getting caught. Anyway, it's what he wants. For now. And that's fine. We can give him that. I can give him that, if it makes him feel better. But it's not how I want things for the long term... So, I have to ask. What do *you* want for the long term?" He stares straight into my eyes.

"The way I understand things, in the long term, I'm going to be CEO of Lennox Breweries."

"I wouldn't be so sure of the length of that term," Sebastian says. He gets up and pours himself another drink. "Do you want a beer? I have a fridge full of Lennox lager that will never be drunk by anyone."

"How very kind of you." I go to the kitchen—a clinically stark, white affair also—and grab myself a beer. It gives me some time to think about Sebastian's comment. I will have to tell Jill about this, but for now, I need to make a quick decision on my own. "I know you want to run the company as well as be the face of it, but you're going to have to step back for a bit. It's the way things are. That being said..." I take a sip from my beer. "Nothing is set in stone. You're my brother. We can work together." I quash the memory of the conversation with Jill—the one where I said I'd like him to go.

Sebastian nods. He seems to have forgotten about the coke on his coffee table. "I'm glad we're on the same page."

A silence falls again. My thoughts drift to Leah, and I wonder if Sebastian's thinking of her as well. Is she still his first thought in the morning, before he opens his eyes, before he's fully awake to the reality of our lives without her—forever?

When we were kids, after Leah and I graduated from finding our cute little brother super adorable, our favorite pastime was to gang up on him. Sebastian had no recourse against his pair of older sisters.

"Are you seeing anyone?" I ask. There are no signs of any regular female presence in my brother's apartment.

"Yeah. Sure," he says absent-mindedly, as though I've just asked him if he wants to order some food.

"Tell me about her."

He looks at me and, for a split second, I spot the forlorn look in his eyes, the same one he used to get when Leah and I went too far with him when we were kids. His gaze turns hard again. "There's nothing to tell. She's just... It's nothing serious. I don't seem to attract a lot of serious girls."

Same here, I want to say, but it has never really bothered me. And it's not something I want to bond over with my brother.

"Dad was fifty years old when I was born," Sebastian says. "I figure I have some time to start a family."

"He hasn't put pressure on you to produce some Lennox grandkids?"

Sebastian shakes his head. "Grandkids don't really seem to interest him that much."

"Figures," I say. "He never had much time for his own children when they were growing up, either."

"Harsh." Sebastian briefly arches his eyebrows.

"Do you want to grab some dinner or something?" I ask.

He shakes his head again, looking more dejected than I've seen him in a while. "I have a date," he says.

"I'll get going then." I don't finish my beer. I used to pretend Lennox beer was the best in the world, but there's no need for such pretense here. Sebastian just stocks it in his fridge for show.

6

JILL

"He's not going to go down easy, if that's what you were expecting," Ali says.

I'm surprised she's relaying her conversation with Sebastian in such detail. I'm also very pleased with how she's confiding in me.

"I wasn't expecting that at all." I give Ali a thorough once-over. The overly colorful floral pattern of her blouse is making my eyes hurt, but at least she doesn't look hungover today. Her large brown eyes are on full display.

"I was thinking," Ali says. "Although I *love* your idea of me spending time in this company's various departments, I shouldn't neglect my time with you, Jill. After all, you can teach me the most."

"Don't worry, you won't be neglected." Sometimes, when I look at Ali, I wonder what her sister would have looked like at this age. For fraternal twins, they always looked very alike.

"I was also thinking..." Sounds as though Ali has been thinking non-stop. It makes a nice change. "Not to sound overly morbid, but, you know, Dad's not in the best shape...

what if something happens to him, say, next week. What happens then?"

"If you've already been announced as his successor, then you'll take over as CEO."

Ali scoffs. "But how would that even be possible? I don't… you know, have enough… information."

As she is now, in the grip of doubt, her Lennox obnoxiousness toned down, I can even summon some compassion for her. "I'll be here. I have all the *information* you need."

She nods and as she does the look in her eyes goes from hesitant to confident again. "What's on your schedule today?"

"Why?" I'm already not liking the sound of that—Ali's tone is too provocative.

"I think it's time for an exercise in trust. You know, me learning to trust Jill Gold." She paints on a big smile. It's broad and mellow, yet I still can't tell whether it's genuine.

"That's going to have to wait until after work. I'm far too busy today."

Ali squints and holds my gaze. "I do wonder how many times per day you avail of the 'I'm busy' excuse just because it's convenient."

"I am really busy, Ali." And you following me around, asking questions like this, isn't reducing said busyness, I think. Perhaps I should be able to say it out loud, but Ali is still the boss's daughter.

"Fine. Tonight then?"

"Tonight what?" On a good day, I don't leave the office before eight. On a regular day, I'm here until ten. On bad days, which are frequent, I often see the clock turn to midnight.

"I'm not sure yet, but I'll think of something. Shall we say seven?"

"Can you be a bit less vague?" I hear footsteps outside the door. Linda is probably waiting to update me on the latest.

"I'm sorry, but I can't yet. All I can say is that it will be a trust-building activity." She waggles her eyebrows. "Shall we meet in the lobby?"

"Ali, I'm really busy today. Seven is just not doable."

"How about..." She walks toward me. "You make it work? It's important that we trust each other, wouldn't you agree?"

I'll have to return to the office for another late-night shift after whatever Ali will plan for us, but it's not as if I have to cancel any exciting non-work activities for it.

"Fine. I'll be there."

"I look forward to it." Ali cocks her head. "Am I still in market research today?" She fills her cheeks with air. "Market research is turning out to be excruciatingly boring."

"You are. Now go. I'm sure someone there is waiting for you." I make a mental note to check in with Jim, the head of the department, to see how Ali's doing.

"See ya." She gives me a quick wave goodbye.

"We're having dinner?" I ask. It sounds like a silly question because she's just handed her car keys to the valet of a restaurant called Matriciana's.

"It's not what it looks like." She nods her head in the direction of the door.

I follow her inside. It looks like a restaurant to me, and not even a very posh one. Not one I had expected Ali Lennox to frequent. Instead of asking for a table, she escorts me to the hallway that branches off the main room, and then down a flight of purple-painted wooden stairs.

When we are in the basement, she knocks on a closed door. I hope she's not taking me to a high-stakes poker game—I'm severely out of practice.

The door swings open and a man with his hair tied into a shiny bun on top of his head gives her a quick once-over.

"The password's Ali Lennox," she says, shooting man-bun a smile.

"Come on in." The man opens the door wide and ushers us in. He takes us to a booth with leather benches that's tucked into a snug alcove.

"It's a speakeasy," Ali says. "It's all the rage. Like alcohol-free beer, although there's no shortage of alcohol here." She wrinkles her nose. "I bet they serve virgin cocktails here as well. Whatever tickles your fancy, Jill."

"A speakeasy." I glance around, although my view is half obstructed, which is probably the intention. The space is roomy but with low ceilings. As far as I can see, there are only five other booths like ours. "What's with the password?"

"You normally get it from some social media account, but me being me, I can usually just say my name to get in. It opens many a door." She says it as though it's the most normal thing in the world. To her, it probably is. Doors have always opened for Ali without her having to make any effort.

"You brought me to a cocktail bar?" I peer at her over the frame of my glasses.

"You do still like a tipple?"

Oh yes, I do. I nod. "It's just not what I had expected."

"Let's order and then I'll tell you more of what I have in mind." She beckons the server over with the slightest nod of her head. "What do you like in your mixed alcoholic beverages, Jill?"

"Something strong." I have a feeling I'm going to need it. "Bourbon."

"It'll be the best bourbon-based cocktail you've ever had."

Ali places our order, then fixes her gaze on me. "I hope you weren't expecting one of those weird trust-building exercises where we fall backward into each other's arms. I think it's too soon for that, actually. Also, I'm not sure you could catch me."

"I can assure you that I could." She has me on edge already.

None of the staff at Lennox Breweries who are Ali's age have her almost-grotesque confidence. They don't even come close.

"Maybe we can try that later, then." She grins at me. "Full disclosure, I googled trust-building activities and the first thing that I found was that we should tell each other a secret. That's why I brought you here. Wouldn't you say the vibe is very conducive to the sharing of secrets?"

For someone interning in the market research department, Ali's research skills haven't reached great depths just yet. What I am impressed with is the unwavering straightforwardness with which she addresses me. She's nothing like the skinny pile of sadness that left L.A. after Leah died—a blow as hard for Ali as the car crash that killed Leah. Somehow, she pulled herself up by the bootstraps and remade herself, without her twin.

"Secrets," I say. "Okay." I can tell Ali plenty of things she will consider to be a secret, but will have zero repercussions on either of our lives if she knows them.

"First, we drink, of course." She glances around. The server is just coming over with our drinks. If he hadn't been on his way, I suspect Ali might have made a condescending snapping noise with her fingers to hurry things along.

She waits until the server has deposited our drinks on the table, informed us my cocktail is called a 'Divided Sky' and has left. Ali lifts her glass and tips it toward mine. "To the future of LB. May it be in female hands." She casts a glance at my hands, as though to make a point as to whose she's referring to—alongside hers, of course. Currently, I don't hold any future in them, only a very enticing-looking cocktail. It has the thinnest slice of burnt orange carefully placed over the rim of the glass.

"To your return." I smile at Ali. For all the years I've worked alongside her brother, he has never invited me for an after-work drink.

"It's good to be back." She shrugs. "You can't run away forever."

I'm taken aback by her sudden candor. But if we'll be exchanging secrets soon, perhaps it shouldn't surprise me.

We sip from our drinks. Mine is indeed exquisite. It's dangerous because I can barely taste the alcohol even though any bourbon-based cocktail I've had has always left me a little giddy.

"Sebastian's stint in rehab hasn't worked," she half-whispers. "I don't know if him going there was purely for PR reasons or whether Dad expected it to actually have an effect."

"Mainly PR," I say, noticing how jaded that sounds. Perhaps I've spent too much time with this family. "I mean, it would have been great if it *had* worked, but I imagine Sebastian isn't feeling too great at the moment with the way things are going."

"He threw a bag of coke on the table last night. As though it were a packet of mints. He didn't offer any to me, nor did he use it in front of me, but for some reason, it was important to him that I see he had it." She knits her brows together. "I can't really read him on that front. He wasn't an addict when I left."

"Sebastian's biggest problem is that he thinks he can do whatever he likes. Until your father sets him straight. Then he'll be good, or pretend to be good, for a while, until it spirals out of control again."

"If that's the case..." She pouts her lips. "Instead of trying to fuck him over, shouldn't we be helping him? I don't much care to have another sibling die on me."

Again, Ali's candidness stuns me into momentary silence.

"We will help him. Of course, we will. But we can't have him leading the company, not in the state he's in."

"He basically said I was a coward for leaving him and Dad to deal with Leah's death without me." She gives that one-shouldered shrug again.

"We all deal with a tragedy like that differently," I say. "For what it's worth, your father doesn't think you're a coward."

"Let's get to the order of business." She sits up straighter, ignoring the direction our conversation has taken. "I've had a few more hours to think about this, so I'll go first."

"Sure." Despite having had no time to prepare, I already know the secret I'm going to tell Ali. I try to guess what she's going to say, or if she can surprise me at all, only to realize, with a shock, that I'm quite excited about this whole thing she has set up.

"When I was a kid… maybe eight or nine—Mom had been dead for a few years—I used to sneak out of the house at night and go looking for her. Spoiler alert: I never found her." She gazes into her half-empty cocktail glass.

If I was taken aback by her frankness earlier, I'm currently floored by her vulnerability on display.

"I'm so sorry you had to go through that, Ali."

"At least I had Leah. Until I didn't."

I'm beginning to see that Ali hasn't brought me here to pry some secret out of me. I'm here, in this dark, underground bar, to see her pain. She's trusting me for some reason. Or her pain is still so big that she can't keep it inside, despite her image, built-up while abroad, of being forthwith and carefree.

This is a situation I don't know how to deal with. Give me a difficult contract negotiation any day of the week. Heck, put me on the losing end of a killer deal over this. Now, I just sit across from Ali wishing I could take away only a fraction of the loss she has come back to face.

"You two were inseparable," I manage to mumble.

"To tell you the truth, she got on my nerves a lot as well. She was always… *there,* you know. Like she couldn't do anything without me."

And vice versa. When Leah died, so unexpectedly and way too early at twenty-five, it must have felt like a limb was ripped from Ali's body, leaving nothing but painful emptiness in the space it used to occupy.

"Ali." I find myself half-whispering as well, as though these things can't possibly be said with a full voice. "It must have been so hard, but if only you could see yourself now."

"Do go on..." She has pulled one side of her mouth into a grin.

"Your presence is..." I speak slowly so I can choose my words. "Very imposing. You're elegant and smart and well-spoken. You look as though you're doing really well."

"Thanks," she says, as though I just complimented her on a piece of jewelry. She downs the rest of her cocktail. "Shall we get another?"

"Sure." I can't say no now, not after Ali has let me in like that. A small part of me can't help but wonder if she's playing me in some way. Vile as it may sound, in my job, I need to be vigilant about these things. For all I know, she and Sebastian could have had a reconciliatory night and forged their own plans to oust me. But would Ali really use her grief like that?

The fact is that I don't know. This is not the same girl who left at the age of twenty-five. No person is the same ten years later, and especially not someone who lost their twin sister in a completely senseless road accident.

She does that thing again where she beckons over someone to wait on her without me noticing, like she has a secret, invisible language going on with the staff. The server doesn't even come over to take our order. The mixologist just goes to work pouring liquor.

"Okay," Ali says. "I feel like we've veered off course a bit. It wasn't my intention to be so, um, open about things with you. I don't know why I did that. Maybe because I feel like I've known you forever. I don't know. How long have you worked for my dad? Twenty-five years?"

I chuckle. "No. I'm not *that* old."

"How old are you?"

"Just turned fifty-three."

"Oh," she says. "Five-three, the opposite of my three-five."

"I've been with Lennox twenty-one years, but I haven't always worked so closely with your father."

"Yet, I seem to remember you always being there."

"That's probably because I was there from the time you started showing interest."

She shrugs again, indicating she doesn't much care to delve deeper into my history at Lennox.

"Anyway." She looks me straight in the eye. "Would you say that I've earned the right to ask you a direct question?"

I'm saved by man-bun bringing over our freshly mixed drinks, but then he's gone, and I have to admit that, yes, she has earned that right.

"Shoot," I say, and hold up my drink.

"Are you a lesbian?" Ali's voice is smooth and bright, not a hint of hesitation lurking in her tone.

"That's hardly a secret."

"Is that a yes?"

"Well, yes. I'm a lesbian. Always have been."

"You say it so casually, yet it's not talked about at Lennox."

"Why would it be? It's my personal life. Therefore, it's private."

"Has my father ordered you in some way, direct or not, to never mention it?"

"What?" Not even Jeffrey would stoop that low. "No. It's just not something that I shout from the rooftops."

"It seems more than that. It almost feels like you want to keep it very much hidden." She tilts her head. "What's the big deal? I'm a lesbian. I wouldn't be surprised if Sebastian had slept with his fair share of men. No one of my generation really cares about those boundaries anymore."

"So?" I'm not entirely sure what I'm being interrogated about.

"I just—I don't know. I don't get your stance on the whole thing."

"I don't get what you're asking me, Ali. Yes, I'm a lesbian. There's nothing further to say."

"I must have known that about you before I left, yet it only occurred to me the other day when you were pouting because I was late. It just came back to me, in a flash. And it just seemed so... *undisclosed*."

"It's not a secret. I don't know what more I can say."

"You're not one of those self-loathing lesbians, are you? You know, because of your generation or something like that?"

"My *generation*?" I shake my head.

"Do you have a partner? A wife you keep hidden in your Hollywood mansion?"

"Firstly, I don't live in Hollywood. Secondly, I'm single."

Ali regards me in silence. "There's so much I don't know about you, Jill." She narrows her eyes. "Have I offended you?"

"Was it your intention to offend me?"

"No. Absolutely not. I just wanted to know."

"Now you do." I return Ali's gaze, still unsure of what this is. Maybe she wants to know about her father's reaction to it, but I told him years ago, as a quick and simple aside one late night, and we never discussed it again. It's not the sort of relationship we have. And I've never had much to discuss. As far as I'm aware, Jeffrey never made a big deal out of anyone's sexuality, aside from the occasional joke in poor taste. I'm guessing that even Jeffrey knows when to count his lucky stars when it comes to what is left of his family.

"Now I do." Ali pulls her lips into a full-blown smile, as though the sole purpose of her evening has been fulfilled.

7

ALI

I HAVE no idea what game I'm playing with Jill. All I know is that I'm enjoying it immensely. I don't even know why I said those things about Leah and my mother. Although I've always made a point of mentioning them—of honoring their lives instead of pretending that their deaths didn't change mine forever.

Jill's wearing a turtleneck again. Today, it's navy. It seems overly rigid and formal in the looser atmosphere of the bar. While living in hot and humid climates in the east, I recognized the importance of protecting yourself against the continuous blast of air-conditioning, but it feels, somehow, as though Jill is hiding something underneath that abundance of clothes. I'd expected her to change from her office wear before coming out with me this evening, but no. It's like she wants to hide her body. And she's already so tiny. Standing next to her, I feel like a giant. It makes it hard to follow her instructions at the office, yet she gets to boss me around. Maybe that's why I'm doing this. It's always fun to mess with the boss. I'm also doing it, I realize when I take in the rest of her features, just because I can.

If my sister's untimely death has taught me anything, it's to do as much of what I damn well please as possible. For all I know, I might crash my car tomorrow, and die. Life is nothing more than something ultra-fragile we can barely hold on to.

Jill's features are delicate, her skin smooth. When she gestures with her hands however, which she does a lot, it's always measured, as if even the movements of her hands shouldn't take up too much space. She's compact and to the point, making me wonder if she modeled her demeanor after her stature or whether it happened naturally.

"Thanks for telling me," I say, while trying to gauge what she's thinking. What must she think of me? This spoiled brat swooping in on her turf. Because management of Lennox Breweries is very much her domain. But I'm not done yet. I have one more pressing question that demands an immediate reply. "You are planning on coming to my party this weekend, aren't you? You're not allowed to duck out."

She chuckles. "Wow. You are relentless. Cocktails in the middle of the week. House party on Saturday. I'm not three-five anymore, Ali. At the weekend, I need my rest."

"Bullshit."

To Jill's credit, she doesn't flinch at my colorful use of language. She's been my father's number two for too long to mind.

"How would you know? You don't know what my life is like," she says. The fight in her comes out more when she's had a few. Or maybe she's relaxing more around me as times goes on.

"You're right, but… don't forget what's at stake." I send her a smile. I only notice now how very blue her eyes are.

"Look, Ali." She sips from her cocktail. "I understand that your trust is something that I have to earn, but I don't see how I could possibly do that by showing up at a party of thirtysomethings getting wasted. That's not my scene. That's not relaxing to me."

"And yet... you said you'd come."

"I did," she admits.

"Do you mean you're not a woman of your word?"

She shakes her head. I don't detect any wariness in her glance yet. Maybe she's enjoying this as much as I am. Surely, Jill knows how to play this game—this plying of the boss's child. God knows what she's had to do to keep Sebastian happy all those years I was gone.

"No. In fact, you won't find many people at Lennox who are truer to their word than I am. What I'm saying is there are other ways for you to learn to trust me—or get to know me if you will. Because that's what it comes down to in the end."

"Fair enough." Jill can sound very convincing. "How about if I promised you it would be a small, intimate gathering? Not some wild, pool-party extravaganza. You can even wear one of your turtleneck sweaters."

She brings her hand to the collar of her navy sweater, as though she had forgotten she was wearing it. "I'm always cold for some reason."

"Even in L.A."

"I thought when I moved here from the east coast, I'd always be pleasantly warm, and I am much warmer than I used to be, but this wretched air-conditioning everywhere..."

Maybe, I think, these are the moments in which I'll get to know more of Jill Gold. These interludes when she lets her guard fully down and just articulates what's running through her head at the time.

"How about," Jill says, "instead of having me over at your house for a party with other people, I take you to dinner tonight. I'm starving and these"—She taps a short but manicured nail against her cocktail glass—"are starting to go to my head."

"Tempting," I say, holding her gaze. "Unfortch, I have plans."

"Really? You're going out after this?"

"I'm young and single and I just got back to L.A." As though that's enough of an explanation. But I don't owe Jill any explanations.

"No hangover in the office tomorrow."

"Yes, boss."

"Don't you need to eat something before you go on elsewhere?" she asks. Is she so keen to take me to dinner? It's not that I don't want to have dinner with her—the evening has been pleasant enough so far. But I want to see how she'll hold herself at my house, being forced to mingle with my friends. It's important for me to observe her out of her comfort zone.

"Don't worry. I'll eat something." I take a deep swallow, finishing the last of my cocktail. "And I won't be hungover tomorrow, I promise. As long as you don't renege on our quid pro quo."

"Fine, Ali. I'll come to your house if it's so important to you." She stares into my eyes, as though she can find the answer as to why I want her there so badly in them. "But that's it. The quid pro quo ends there. I will prove to you in other ways that you can trust me—in fact, I'm quite convinced you'll learn to do so by working with me. And, well, there's also the matter of me trusting you, of course." She cocks her head. "As far as I know, you and Sebastian might be plotting to remove me from LB."

"Yeah, right. Have you met my brother?" I suppose she has to live with a certain degree of paranoia in her job.

"I know him all too well. He's had some issues, but he's bright and he can be ruthless. Don't underestimate him, Ali. I don't."

I just nod. I don't need a lesson on my brother's personality. I grew up with him. But Jill has spent more time with him these past ten years.

"Has he screwed you over at work?" I have to ask.

"He has most certainly tried." Jill doesn't elaborate.

"I'm not planning anything with Sebastian," I say matter-of-factly. "But you're right. Trust is a two-way street." I gesture to the server to bring me the check.

8

JILL

JUST GETTING to Silver Lake has already been a pain in the ass. And after Ali's comment about my sweater the other night, I've tried to make a sartorial effort, eschewing my trusted sweaters and wearing a light blouse instead.

It's not difficult to find Ali's house. Although modest in size for a Lennox property, it's lit up brightly and loud music is thumping through a battery of speakers. So much for small and intimate. She must have decided to not go with that plan then.

Also very un-Lennox-like is the absence of any security. I can just waltz into Ali's house without my name being checked off any list. Maybe she has invited the entire neighborhood to this shindig and everyone can just walk in and out as they please.

In a way, I do admire her lack of paranoia. Maybe living abroad has done her a world of good. And of course, there's no shortage of staff milling about the place, serving drinks and canapés. Ali wasn't going to do that herself. Maybe they've been asked to keep an eye on things. As I walk through the front yard, I realize I'm the one with paranoia issues. I grab a glass of champagne from a passing tray and lurk outside for a bit.

None of the servers are offering Lennox beers, although I do see some people sipping from bottles. I decide to circumvent the house and make my way to the back yard via the side. The instant I see the pool I want to turn around and flee.

I think of my apartment downtown. The reading chair I like to curl into on a Saturday night, when, at least sometimes, I'm free of work expectations. When I was getting ready, I amped myself up by repeating that this was just another work thing. Now that I'm here, though, with all those half-naked bodies in the pool, and the average age of the people around me less than half of mine, it feels more like psychological torture.

And where is Ali, anyway? I just want to say hello and get out of here. I sip from the champagne—Ruinart, her father's favorite as well—and move a little farther into the garden.

"You must be Jill." A young woman in shorts and a painfully colorful shirt has sidled up to me. "I'm Madison. Ali's BFF." She holds out the hand that's not holding a bottle of beer. Inadvertently, I check if it's one of ours—it isn't.

I shake her hand, which seems very formal for the occasion. "I am."

"The guest list got a little out of hand at the last minute," Madison says. "You know how it goes."

"Do I?" Oh, I said that out loud.

Madison just sniggers. "Ali likes a party. She likes to celebrate life, you know? What with all she's been through."

I just nod. I have no opinion on Ali's partying ways. And Madison might be the nicest woman in Los Angeles, but I don't feel much like making small talk with her. Unless Ali has told her to look out for my arrival—assuring her I would stick out like a sore thumb—and has tasked her with submitting me to some sort of test.

"Where is Ali?" I ask.

"Playing the hostess with the mostest, I think. She can get a bit hyper when she throws a party."

"Being her... BFF," I turn fully toward Madison so I can read her face, "do you have any idea why it's so important to Ali that I be here? You and I can both see that I don't really fit in."

Madison shrugs. She looks like the kind of girl who sleeps in, drives her truck to the beach, and catches waves all day. In the evening, she goes to parties like these.

"Knowing Ali, she's probably just fucking with you. Is she trying to get back at you for something?" She pulls her lips into a lop-sided grin.

"Not that I'm aware of, but the fucking-with-me part makes sense." I drink some more champagne.

"Now that you're here, why don't you make yourself comfortable?" She looks around—perhaps for a space where she could make me feel more comfortable. "Come with me."

She guides us to a cluster of deck chairs far away enough from the pool to avoid splatter. She sits on one and I do the same. As soon as I finish my glass of champagne, it's replaced by another, making it feel like a quintessential Lennox party, where every detail has been agonized over. On the other hand, it's very far removed from any party I've ever been to since I turned forty.

"Can you do me a favor, Madison?"

"Of course." She flashes me a grin again.

"Can you tell Ali I was here? I think I might leave now."

"Say what?" Madison narrows her eyes. "You only just arrived."

"I'm well aware, but now I'd like to leave."

"Nah, come on, Jill." Madison fixes her gaze on me. "Stay a while." It sounds more like an order than a suggestion. But I won't let myself be bossed around by Ali Lennox's BFF—or minion, more like. I don't want to be here and that's the end of that. "At least finish your drink before you order a ride. Give us five more minutes of your time."

I sit next to Madison in silence for a while. I have no clue what to say to her and she seems content to let her gaze swoop over the impossibly beautiful people in the pool. I feast my eyes on what's going on in front of me as well. It's not just the effortless beauty of youth that strikes me about the throng of people huddled around an inflatable unicorn. It's their ease, their almost blatant self-confidence, something I see in Ali as well. And, now, also in Madison. They all look as though nothing in the world can ever hurt them.

"How long have you known Ali?" I ask, eventually. I feel like I need to reward Madison in some way for sticking with me and conversation is all I have to offer—a few questions to indicate that I'm interested in finding out more about her.

"Forever." She giggles. When I see a man in the far corner of the pool taking a long drag from a joint, I realize Madison is probably under the influence herself.

All the more reason to get out of here. I hope Sebastian wasn't invited. This isn't the kind of party that would be conducive to his recovery, although both Ali and I know that his recovery is just a front to keep his father happy.

I let a few minutes go by, then get up, and try to slip away. Madison grabs me by the wrist, and says, "It was lovely meeting you, Jill."

"Likewise," I mumble, and take a deep breath. Even though I can't trust Madison to assure Ali I was actually at her party, I have the visual imagery of it etched into my brain. An exact description of what her back yard looked like at twenty to ten should convince Ali I was actually here. I briefly consider heading into the house and trying to find her, just to say a quick hello—I did come all this way—but decide against it when I see the flock of people hanging out in the kitchen.

As I retrace my steps to the front garden, I get a few funny looks from people, but nothing I can't deal with. I've almost made it to the front gate when I hear a familiar voice behind me.

"Hey," Ali says. "Where do you think you're going, Jill?"

9

ALI

I've managed to convince Jill to come inside and we sit in the living room, away from most of the guests. There's not much point in scolding her for trying to slink off without even saying hello to me. Her body language screams that she'd rather be anywhere else but here. I thought I'd get more of a kick out of seeing her like that, but as it turns out, I feel a little bit sorry for her. She's not the only person present here who's above a certain age, but this is not about age. This is about personality and this party couldn't suit Jill Gold's personality less. She's not a go-with-the-flow kind of person, it would appear.

She has dressed in a silk blouse instead of her usual sweater. It should make her look more relaxed—less in work mode—but it doesn't.

"I should have taken you up on that dinner invitation," I say.

"I get that you're very, very used to getting what you want, Ali. And you needed me to show up here tonight to exert some imaginary dominance over me. And it's fine, you know. I'm here. It's just some time I've lost. But don't go making a habit out of doing this because I will soon have had enough of it."

It's not the first time Jill sees right through me—even better than I can see through myself. Her ability to do so intrigues me. If she's such a connoisseur of people, why has she been working for a heartless bastard like my father for more than two decades? Or perhaps, although she's learned to read people for who they really are, she's also learned not to judge them. Maybe that's Jill's secret superpower.

"Got it." No use playing coy now. And Jill is such a good sport. She let me take her out last Wednesday and she showed up tonight. I can't ask more of her. In a way, it's more than I've been given by someone Lennox-related in a very long time. "Now that you're here, do you want a tour of the house?"

"Sure, but let me order a car first," she says. "I'll let them know to pick me up in fifteen minutes."

I don't protest.

"This is where the magic happens," I say, foolishly, when I show Jill my bedroom. Not a lot of magic has happened since I moved back to L.A., despite me sometimes telling Madison otherwise.

Jill doesn't look very impressed. I assume it's my words that are underwhelming and not the decoration of my bedroom, in which no other guests are allowed tonight.

"Oh wow," she says when she sees the childhood picture of Leah and me, taken on the deck of the Malibu beach house my mother loved so much.

In the picture, Leah and I look as though we love our surroundings as well. We still had a mother then, after all. Leah still had more than twenty years to live.

"It's the first thing I see every morning." I always say good morning to my sister, as if she's still alive and just woke up in the bed next to me.

"Does it... help?" Jill keeps her eyes glued to the picture.

"I guess. Otherwise I would probably move the picture."

"It's strange." Jill leans against the wall. "I'm so much older than you are, yet I've not had to deal with a major loss like that."

"You're not that much older."

"Still," Jill says. "A lot of people my age have had family and close friends pass away. I've been spared that."

I realize I know nothing of Jill's family and I'm also left to wonder if she has many close friends. All she does, from what I gather, is work.

"That being said, I do know..." She doesn't continue.

"What?"

She looks at the picture again. Leah and I must have only been three years old. Our smiles are wide and goofy. Sebastian had just been born. All those years that have passed, I think. Sebastian had to fake his way through rehab and I'm somehow getting my kicks luring Jill to a house party she would never have enjoyed, perhaps not even in her twenties or thirties. She seems a bit too uptight for that, although I could be wrong. Maybe she hasn't always been a turtleneck-wearing workaholic.

"What were you going to say?" I sidle closer to her.

"Nothing." She waves off my question. "I think it's very moving that you keep this picture here. It says something about you that isn't always obvious."

"What's that supposed to mean?"

"I think you know, Ali." She doesn't smile, just tilts her head a little and stares at me in a peculiar way. It's an expression I don't really know what to do with.

The DJ in the garden turns up the bass and it thumps through me. It's as though the revved up music intensifies the heat of the alcohol in my blood and I lose my balance for a fraction of a second. I steady myself against the wall and find myself face-to-face with Jill.

"Are you taking care of yourself, Ali?" Jill asks. "All these parties… is that really what you want?"

I scoff. She may be able to read me correctly half of the time, but the other half, she can be so wrong. "What are you talking about? I love this."

"Okay." She puts a hand on my bare shoulder. It takes me aback because I can't remember the last time my father has hugged me—maybe when my mother died, but that was so long ago, I hardly remember. Certainly not when Leah died. Then, he just wrapped himself in a stone-cold silence. And yet Sebastian wondered why I had to leave. "Remember, I have your back, okay? If there's anything you need, you let me know."

I'm touched by her outpouring of concern. Maybe that's why I really wanted her here tonight. Because I know that, in her own way, she cares about me. And she's easy to talk to. I confide in Jill easily. She represents something that I've missed. Something a friend can't give. She's close enough to my family to understand, yet removed enough to not be part of the stubborn silence us Lennoxes adhere to when it comes to our emotions. And she's a woman. A familiar woman. Someone who has always been there. Someone, I know, without having to play any games or put her to some foolish test, I should instinctively trust.

"Thank you," I say, and I mean it from the bottom of my heart.

I take a step closer and, under my sister's celluloid gaze, I lean forward. Without giving it any further thought, my mind blank and hotly spurred on by her kind words, I press my lips to hers.

She pulls back immediately. "What the f—"

"Oh, shit. Oh, no, Jill. No, I didn't mean to." *Oh, fuck.*

Jill shakes her head. All the kindness that was present in her gaze just moments earlier has left. I see nothing but disdain for the spoiled brat who always just goes after what she wants without taking others people's feelings into account.

"I'm sorry," I mutter.

Jill's phone beeps. "My car's here." She sends me one last disapproving look, then dashes out of the door and down the stairs.

Why did I do that? It's not a question I can answer without the help of a few bottles of champagne.

10

JILL

How dare she? The three words keep flashing through my mind, thumping through my veins. How dare she invite me to her garish party with too much booze and drugs, lure me to her room, where I was sure to see that picture of Leah and her, and feel subsequently sorry for her, and kiss me?

Thank goodness my car has arrived. I slide into the back and sit there fuming as the lights of the Los Angeles night flicker outside.

This can only be explained by Ali's unbelievable, grotesque privilege. I was nice to her—genuinely nice. Perhaps a sensation she doesn't get to experience very often. And her confused, still-grieving mind took it for something else. For goodness' sake. How am I going to work with her now?

Maybe we should pretend it never happened. No. That's the Lennox way. We will talk about it. She will apologize more. And we'll move on. I was too shocked to examine her features, but she did look very sorry. She'd probably drunk too much. Or shared the joint that made Madison high.

Just one of those nights, I mumble to myself. The worst of the shock has subsided and, as we hurtle down Sunset, I realize

I'm actually not that shocked by Ali's inappropriate behavior. Not only because she's a Lennox, but because of the generation she's part of. The *I'll-have-that-right-now* generation.

I tell myself that I can easily shake this off. This doesn't have to impede our plans to take the reins at Lennox. But it does make me realize that I need Ali more for that than she needs me. Although she needs me too, if only to ward off Sebastian. It's only together that we can beat him for control over Lennox.

I take a few deep breaths and then allow myself to follow a different train of thought. Regardless of her psychological motivation behind it, her obvious vulnerability and sensitivity, why would Ali, who could go out into the night and kiss any woman she wanted, kiss me?

I have no response to that, except circumstance and context, which will have to do for now.

On Sundays, I always try to ban thoughts of anything work-related and, instead, enjoy what I call my private life. Perhaps I should make more effort to turn it into something vibrant and joyful, but that will have to wait until at least next week. This particular Sunday, I can't get Ali out of my head. So much for trying to move on.

Because I'm agitated, I scroll through the *Financial Times* newsfeed. Equally, on Sundays, I try to avoid the news, because it always sets my thoughts off into a direction that's the opposite of relaxed. I should go for a hike. Or go see a movie. Or maybe I should do some cooking. I find myself walking around my apartment, not knowing what to do with myself.

When my phone rings, I hope it's work. Who else could it be?

It's Ali.

I consider not picking up at first, but the ring is so insistent, so pleading, a bit like the look in her eyes last night. The girl whose party was raging downstairs while she was looking at a picture of her dead sister. So of course, I pick up.

"Jill." Ali's voice is hesitant. There's nothing of her millennial self-possessed confidence in it. "I—um, can I see you? I just... I don't know. I'm so sorry. I feel I need to apologize to you as soon as possible so we can put this behind us. I don't—"

"Ali, calm down." This is a girl who hasn't had a mother since she was five, I remind myself. "It's fine," I lie. "It never happened. Okay?"

"Can we meet before we see each other at the office tomorrow?" she asks, suddenly eloquent again.

It might not be a bad idea. This is not the kind of energy I want to waltz into work with. Best to get rid of it as quickly and swiftly as possible. "Sure. Let's meet today."

"I'll come to you. Can you text me your address, please? I'll leave within the next half hour."

Now it sounds as though I no longer have any say in the matter. "Okay. See you in a bit."

When we hang up, I do as instructed and text Ali my address. It should take her at least half an hour to get here from Silver Lake. I glance around my living room but, most days, I don't spend enough time in it to create any sort of mess. I do see the irony in working for a large paycheck to afford a beautiful home but working too much to spend any significant time enjoying it. At least Ali threw a party at her house. When was the last time I had people over? I have to strain my memory and I still can't come up with an answer—that's how long it has been. Ten more years of this, I tell myself, like I always do. And then I'm through. I'll have plenty of cash stowed away to maintain my standard of living until I'm well past a hundred years old. I'll take up a hobby. Perhaps get a dog and go for long walks. I chuckle. I have no idea what I'll do when I retire.

Maybe I should start looking for someone to share my retirement with. But that's the deal I made with myself. For now, work comes first.

I straighten some things around the apartment and then, before I know it, Ali rings the bell.

11

ALI

When Jill opens the door, I hide my face behind my hands, to show her exactly how sorry I am. And sorry isn't even the worst of it. I mainly feel shame that sits like a heaviness in the pit of my stomach.

"Come in, Ali," she says.

I peek through my fingers first, then let my hands fall away. Jill's not wearing her office turtleneck sweater today—it is Sunday after all. Instead of examining her outfit, my gaze is drawn to the view from her living room window.

"Well fuck me. You can almost see all the way to the ocean."

"Hm," is all she says. I haven't come here to discuss the unexpected expanse of her view. "Can I get you anything? I was expecting to see you more hungover."

"I'm fine. I just, uh, want to get this over with." I sit in the armchair by the large window overlooking the Financial District and beyond it.

"Sure." Jill lowers herself into the couch, which is the same as the one she has in her office. "While it's probably good that you came, let's not make a big deal out of this. I can see it for what it was, you know. We all do crazy impulsive things sometimes that we regret instantly."

"Really? Do you?"

"I most certainly have done. Of course, I have."

As Jill looks at me, her face awash with kindness and understanding, the sensation that overtook me last night threatens to engulf me again. But today, in the daylight, I'm sober and able to not let my emotions guide me. "I'm sorry. It was just so out of line—and out of character. You must think that because I'm a Lennox I just do whatever I want without taking other people's feelings into account. That does happen sometimes, I'll be the first to admit that. I've certainly kissed people who, in hindsight, I shouldn't have gone near. I suffer from poor judgment sometimes, I guess. But last night was just... temporary insanity." I try a smile. "Thanks for being such a good sport about it."

"You don't have to thank me. As far as I'm concerned, it never happened. Okay?"

I nod. But as I do, my eyes are drawn to her lips. They suddenly appear very kissable—again.

"You were emotional," she continues. "And vulnerable."

"And I'd had too much to drink. Way too much." I glance out of the window, away from Jill's pillowy lips. "I just don't want you to think that's why I invited you to my party. It was never my intention."

"Okay. No more party invitations like that, please. I hope we can agree on that."

"I thought we already had." I can feel myself relax a little—as long as I don't look at her face for too long. "No more untowardness from me, I solemnly swear." I let my gaze sweep along her living room. "This place is amazing. Have you lived here long?"

"Must be coming up to seven years now." Jill leans back and folds one leg over the other.

I try to focus on the apartment, which blends modern features with classic furniture so effortlessly, but I do have to look at her once in a while. What will she think if I don't? That I'm not capable? I guess it would illustrate my shame. But, as I sit here, I feel my shame making way for something else.

Jill's dressed in jeans and an even more casual blouse than she wore last night. It's nice to see her neck, I think. Why does she always hide it at work? Is it a symbolic act of protection against corporate vampires?

"Madison was quite taken with you, by the way. She stayed over and this morning you were the main topic of conversation."

"Did you tell her about the kiss?"

Hearing her say the word kiss out loud sends a frisson of something up my spine. She named it. She made it more real. "No. I'm not telling anyone. I don't think that would be a good idea."

"Agreed." Jill leans forward, placing her elbows on her knees. "Look, Ali, if there's ever anything you need to talk about, I'm here. That hasn't changed. I want you to know that."

"For someone so high up at Lennox, you are very kind, Jill. How did you claw your way to the top being like that?" A thought flashes through my head—one I have to push away immediately.

"Contrary to Lennox belief, being nice to people can get you places." She grins at me, but I can't respond.

The thought flashing through my head is so persistent, that my imagination takes over and a slew of very disturbing images is projected in my mind.

"This is going to sound extremely inappropriate and I apologize if I'm off the mark." I shuffle in my seat. "But, um, you and Father haven't, like, you know, had any dalliances over the years?"

"How do you figure that?" Jill says matter-of-factly. "You know I'm a lesbian."

"Well, yes, but sometimes, when certain things are at stake, people can become surprisingly *fluid*."

"What are you suggesting? That despite being a lesbian, I slept with him so I could become COO?" She arches up her eyebrows. "Sometimes I do worry about what goes on in that head of yours."

"When you put it like that, it sounds very offensive. Let's just say my father never honored my late mother's memory. He brought a boatload of often much-younger women into our home. Leah and I used to give him so much flack for it, but in the end, we were just glad that none of them ended up being our stepmother."

"Who cared for you when you were children and your father was at work?"

"Nannies." Jill doesn't seem too offended by what I've just said. I'm pleasantly surprised. She seems to have equal measures of compassion and toughness in her. "Let's see if I can remember… There was Elizabeth. Juanita. Rachel. Connie. Connie Number Two. We even had a Manny once. I think Dad was getting desperate. There were so many. For some reason, they never stuck around." Leah, Sebastian, and I were so spoiled, one of us always found some fault with the person charged with our care. It's hard to please three bereft but privileged children all at once.

I only now notice a series of picture frames on the sideboard next to the window. "Do you mind?" I ask, but I don't wait for her to reply. I get up and walk over to the sideboard and examine the pictures. I feel like I've told Jill quite a bit about myself already. Maybe this is my chance to learn some things about her—perpetually closed book that she is.

"Parents?" I ask. Jill couldn't look more like the two people in the picture. She has her mother's bright blue eyes and her father's asymmetrical mouth.

Jill walks up to me. "Yes."

"Still alive?"

"Oh, yes. Very much so. They're in remarkable health. They live in Montauk. Must be all the sea air that keeps them young."

"We live close to the ocean." I examine the picture further. "How old are they?"

"Eighty and eighty-two," Jill says. She takes the picture from me and a new kind of tenderness burns in her glance.

"They're my father's age. That's so funny... and weird."

My gaze scans over an array of pictures of other people—maybe they're cousins or something—until another picture catches my attention. "Who's this?" In the picture, a twenty-something woman looks candidly into the camera, a bright smile on her face. Her hair is long and black, her eyes mysterious and dark.

"An old friend," Jill says, in a tone that doesn't promise more elaboration.

"What's her name?" I push.

"Melissa." Jill walks away from the sideboard, to the dining table. "Are you sure I can't get you anything?"

It sounds more like: shouldn't you be leaving now?

I know better than to ask more questions about the mystery woman. Although I feel like lingering at Jill's gorgeous apartment a while longer—when sober, I feel so calm and balanced in her presence—I don't want to overstay my welcome.

Before I leave, I have to keep myself from asking if we're still on for dinner sometime soon, but I swallow that question as well. I came here to apologize, after all, not to relentlessly push my luck.

12

JILL

I'M NOT sure why Ali would be so drawn to Melissa's picture, unless she has a secret gift for sniffing out people's weaknesses. I've tried putting the picture away, but it never made me feel any better. On the contrary. It's as though I get satisfaction from punishing myself a little by the sight of her every day—every single time I walk into the living room. That frame has been placed in that spot to catch the maximum amount of attention. Usually, I'm the only one here, though.

Then there was the way Ali looked at me at times, the unintended sparkle in her glance undoing her words of apology. I was more convinced of how sorry she was about kissing me before she turned up at my house.

But I have to take my share of the responsibility as well. Grandiose as it may sound, I've come to believe my presence elicits something in her. It sparks a feeling that has been missing. Perhaps I'm the one who should keep my distance.

I think all of this as I stare at Melissa's picture. It was taken near the end of our affair. Sometimes, I bring the photo close to my face and examine it, looking for the signs that she had already stopped loving me in the tilt of her head, the pull of her lips. But I can't see it. Not now and certainly not then.

I glance at the chair in which Ali sat and an unbearable jumpiness comes over me, an unrest crawling underneath my skin. I need to get out of the house. There are a few places I can go where I won't feel so alone—or should I say lonely?

Insignificant in the grand scheme of things it may be, but one thing Ali's kiss has reminded me of, is exactly how long it's been since a woman pressed her lips against mine. Eighteen months. I don't know where the time has gone since then. I've been working more, perhaps. As Jeffrey's health has declined, my responsibilities have grown. But still. I bet it hasn't been eighteen months since Jeffrey was last kissed.

The thought of that reminds me of Ali's question, which was, in hindsight, extremely inappropriate, yet still understandable. She knows her father and she knows how some women in the company were fast-tracked through promotions, only to be given a generous golden handshake once Jeffrey got fed up with them. For that reason, I can't begrudge her the question. But I like to think Jeffrey has always respected me enough to keep himself from trying anything.

Because I know I'll be drinking, I order a car to pick me up. While I wait, I consider changing into something more glamorous, but it would only make me feel less like myself, which is not how I want to feel when on the prowl.

Fifteen minutes later, I'm on my way to one of my favorite bars. When I first moved to L.A. there were a few lesbian bars left. I've witnessed their demise one by one—not that I frequented any of them regularly. Dolly's is not a lesbian bar, but it's as close as it's going to get in this town. It's also a place where I know I can walk in, no questions asked, and sit by the bar, nursing a drink for as long as I like. And sometimes, I even get lucky. It hasn't been eighteen months since I was last here—and the last time I got lucky, wasn't here either. So maybe my chances for tonight are slim. But that's okay. At least I'm doing something that's not work or sitting at home waiting for a miracle.

Cindy, the owner of Dolly's, greets me with a familiar nod of the head. In the back, a few women are playing pool. Along the bar, all stools are empty except one. I sit on the one as far removed from the other patron as possible.

As I order, I think of the fancy bourbon cocktails I had with Ali last week. There's none of that here. Just bourbon neat or on the rocks.

I place my order and sit, minding my own business. I sit and I wait for something to happen. Once in a while, someone heads to the bar to order some drinks, but nothing else is going on.

The first shot of bourbon relieves the sting of my depressing calculation to eighteen months ago. Her name was Annette. I met her at a cocktail party thrown by one of the shareholders. We ended up in a hotel in mid-town and I try to remember the exact blend of circumstances that made that happen. I'm not one to mix business with pleasure like that, but perhaps, once in a while, even I have no choice.

The second shot of bourbon makes me relive something else. And because of that—because of the sensation of Ali's lips against mine—I order a third shot immediately. Three is always my hard limit, so I savor the last one, while I inwardly berate myself for even thinking about it. It didn't happen, I repeat to myself. But my subconscious doesn't agree. It keeps pushing up new snatches of memory, tiny events it has held on to. First, the surprise when she bent herself toward me, towering over me, really, with her long frame. The scent of flowers coming from her hair. But mostly, and again and again, the softness of her lips. Even though wholly unexpected, there was nothing insistent about the kiss. It was only gentle and probing, as though she was merely trying something out on a whim.

Only until I've finished my third shot of bourbon do I allow myself these thoughts. After that, the only appropriate reaction to them is disgust. This is not a memory to rejoice in. The reasons for that are myriad and I repeat them in my head like a mantra: too young; too damaged; too much the boss's daughter. It's a no-brainer, yet my brain doesn't seem to agree that much.

Once it's clear to me that no one is going to turn up whose affections I can win for the night, I pay my bill, and go home, where there's no one, and nothing waits for me, except more memories of that kiss.

13

ALI

WHAT'S DRIVING me crazy is that I was the one who said to Jill we shouldn't tell anyone. It makes sense that we don't, seeing as we're treating the *incident* as though it never happened. But ever since I told her that, all I want to do is confide in Madison.

Yesterday morning, when I found her sleeping on the couch downstairs, I was still so groggy, the memory hadn't even properly made its way to the forefront of my mind yet. Though it soon caught up with me. Thoughts of Jill's face, that pouty mouth, the deep, kind wells of her eyes, popping out of nowhere, until, through the haze of my hangover, the memory crystallized into a moment of pure torment. Had I really done that? Where on earth had I found the nerve? All I could think of was to call Jill and apologize to her as profusely and as quickly as possible.

I had to sit through brunch with Madison first while my house was being cleaned. As usual on a hungover Sunday, we went to Grizzly's, where, since she's been a regular on television, we can always get a table without me having to explicitly say my name.

Then Madison went on and on about Jill. At first I couldn't

believe it, especially because of the briefness of their interaction, but then I began to accept her sudden infatuation as reality, because I had ended up kissing her myself in my bedroom.

Earlier, Jill didn't as much as flinch when I told her about Madison not being able to shut up about her. It's probably not even a blip on her radar. Maybe she was too busy processing that her boss's daughter had kissed her to pay it much mind. Surely, Jill has far greater worries that need her attention.

Now, I feel that if I don't tell anyone about this soon, I might explode—or worse, the information might explode out of me at a very inopportune moment. I imagine the kiss growing in importance in my mind because of its secrecy and inappropriateness. Growing and growing to such proportions that I can no longer contain it within myself, and, so help me God, blurt it out to Sebastian, of all people, in an unguarded moment.

That can never happen. Being thirty-five, maybe I should be mature enough to keep this to myself and have it blow over. And, despite the persistent memory and the gnawing it does in the back of my brain, resist the urge to tell anyone. Because it meant nothing.

But I know myself. I've always been a talker. I told Leah everything—and vice versa. We had no secrets, even throughout our teens, when we did try to keep them, but they never held because we could always tell when one of us wasn't being completely forthcoming about something. Leah was the first person I told that I liked girls. I was the first person she told about Jimmy Lieberman kissing her in the janitor's closet at school when we were fourteen.

Madison is as close to replacing Leah as I'll ever come. I can't imagine telling anyone else. For all the people who were happy to turn up for my party last night, there was only one of them I trusted to look out for Jill.

So, instead of going home, I drive to Madison's house. I try to remember if she had plans, but knowing her, she'll be catching up on her beauty sleep after last night's debauchery. We're not in our twenties anymore, and she has more than once earned herself a sneer from the make-up artists on set because of her poor complexion on Monday mornings.

I walk around the house to the back garden and find her dozing in a lounge chair by the pool. Lester, her dog, has assumed the almost exact same position in a neighboring chair.

"Wakey-wakey," I whisper.

Madison pulls one eye open. "Ali? Are you okay?"

"Fine. Just checking in on you."

"Why?" She pushes herself up. Lester jumps off his chair to sniff my legs.

With a sigh, I sit where Lester was just napping. "I need to talk to you."

"Sounds ominous." She sits up a little straighter.

"It's nothing serious. But something I thought you should know."

"What? Ali? You're being all mysterious. You know I hate that."

"I didn't have the heart to tell you this morning, but, um… Last night, I kissed Jill."

"Jill Gold? Your boss?" Madison blinks a few times.

I nod.

"Oh come on. And you let me go on and on about her." She juts out her lower lip. "Why did you let me do that?"

"I was still processing."

Madison sighs. "Tell me everything." Her shoulders sag a little.

"There's not that much to tell. Clearly, it was a mistake. I was drunk and we were talking about Leah in my room and before I knew it, I had my lips on hers. It certainly wasn't premeditated. It came completely out of the blue, even for me."

"Damn, Ali. What did she say?"

"She told me off and then she left."

"How did that make you feel?" Madison's eyes have grown a little wider.

"The whole thing confused the hell out of me. So I went to see her earlier and apologized. What else could I do? I told her it was a mistake, of course. A moment of complete lack of judgment. We agreed to, basically, pretend it never happened."

"I can't believe you kissed her," Madison says. "What was it like? The kiss itself, I mean?"

"It was so… fleeting. So quick." If that was the case, I have to ask myself, then why can't I shut up about it?

"What did she say when you went to see her?"

"I think she forgave me for it. She forgave me for making her come to my party as well."

Madison tilts her head. "She didn't have to come."

"I think I may have made it sound as though she really did."

"Still… Maybe, she didn't mind you kissing her all that much."

I shake my head. "No, that's not possible."

"Maybe in your head it's not."

"Stop it, Mads. I have to work with her tomorrow."

"Aren't you interning at various departments?"

"Yes. Thank goodness for that." As much as I dislike my short internships, because not many of my father's employees have the balls to give me actual interesting work to do, tomorrow, I will be glad for them.

"You could also not turn up. What's the worst that will happen?"

"I can't do that." I haven't told Madison about my father wanting to appoint me as the next CEO. I'm under strict orders to tell no one who hasn't been told directly by my father or Jill. Although I could tell Madison. She has kept far worse secrets for me. "My dad," I start. "He wants certain things for me at LB. I need to be there and Jill is mentoring me."

"Since when do you care what Lennox Sr. thinks of you?" Madison reaches for a bottle of water and sips from it.

"It's complicated." I decide not to tell her just yet.

"Then you'll just have to suck it up." She squints at me. "Do you want to go out? Have a few beverages and see what happens?"

"God, no," I groan. "Besides, don't you have an early call time tomorrow?"

"Nope. I don't have to be on set at all tomorrow. So if you do decide to ditch work, we can hang out all day." She reaches out her hand. I take it in my mine.

"I guess I'm growing more responsible with age." And I couldn't bear the disappointed look in Jill's eyes if I turned up at work hungover again.

14

JILL

It's been one of those days where, from the moment I set foot in my office, I don't know where the time has gone. By the time I get ready to leave at eight, more exhausted than usual, I realize I haven't seen Ali all day. This afternoon, I asked Linda to check if she was in and she was—following around Ramon in the marketing department. Another person I need to check in with. But it's too late now. Ramon will have gone home and, frankly, I don't much feel like asking people about how Ali's doing. She has upended my life enough since her father brought her back to head office—and not just my professional life.

I blame Ali for the lingering dull ache throbbing at the back of my skull since I woke up this morning. I shouldn't have gone to Dolly's last night. I got nothing out of it apart from a hangover I really didn't need on a Monday. And a growing sense of loneliness.

Or maybe it was being reminded of Melissa—by Ali asking questions about her. When I got home from Dolly's, I actually opened my laptop and had my fingers hovering over the keyboard, wanting to google her to see what she's up to these days. It's a temptation I've been able to resist for the past few years. Last I heard—and by that, I mean I gleaned from a deep-dive internet search—Melissa is married with children and living in Westchester. I did resist in the end. I was already feeling so down in the dumps, I didn't need to see photos of my ex with her perfect wife and children.

But Ali somehow planted the seed. She made me think of something I'm usually so good at avoiding because I've built my life to make it easy to do so.

"Knock, knock."

I flinch at the sound of her voice.

"Whoa, didn't mean to scare you, Jill."

"I was just lost in thought." I zip up my bag. It's thick with papers I'm taking home to review.

"Off home?"

"What can I do for you?" I make sure my voice sounds like I'm her boss.

"I just wanted to make sure we're good. That there are no hard feelings or any lingering discomfort."

"We're fine," I say curtly. "Although I would appreciate you not mentioning any of this at work."

Every single day, Ali's been dressed in an impressive outfit that could come straight from the catwalk for business attire. It's flamboyant, but still on the edge of appropriate. The blouse she's wearing today has a wide ruffled collar and is so bright green it hurts my eyes.

"All right, Jill." Ali seems to be completely herself again. "It's our secret. But it's important to me that we're okay."

"We're okay."

"Good," she says.

"Fine," I say.

"What are you doing tonight?" she has the audacity to ask.

"Working." I pat my over-stuffed bag.

"Does my father pay you enough for you to be working all the time?"

"He pays me plenty."

"Still... I feel like you should relax more, Jill."

"Ali." I take my bag into my hand, indicating I'm ready to leave. "Is there anything else you need? I'd like to go, please."

"By all means." She steps aside, freeing the doorway.

"Thank you." I wait for her to leave. It's important for my dominance in this relationship, of which I feel I lose a little every time we interact.

"Mind if I walk out with you?"

Yes, I do very much mind is what I should say, but I don't. Of course, I don't. "Sure." I gesture for her to lead the way.

We walk to the elevator in silence.

"The old man has gone for the day, has he?" she asks when we walk past her father's office.

"Do you spend any time with him at home?" I'm suddenly curious.

"You mean at the house?" Ali's words sound as though I've asked her the most improbable question ever.

"Yes. Do you have the occasional dinner or lunch or, I don't know, cocktails?"

"Just me and my dad?" Ali scoffs. "Em, no. We don't have that kind of relationship."

The elevator doors open and we get in. I stand as far away from her as possible.

"What kind of relationship do you have?"

Ali arranges her face into a blank expression. "Honestly, I barely know the man."

"But you have no problem coming to work for him?" I'm not sure why I'm pushing like this—why I want to see Ali out of balance. Maybe it's nothing but a small act of revenge because she has knocked *me* off balance. Not just by kissing me, but by coming to my home, her presence there, somehow, still lingering.

"I'm his eldest child and rightful heir to the throne. Or do you think Sebastian should get it just because he is male?" Ali's definitely not one to take anything lying down. She has the Lennox fighter spirit. And she's much feistier than Sebastian.

"Heavens no, Ali. That you would even think that."

The elevator dings and we arrive in the lobby.

"I don't suppose you want to grab dinner?" She flashes me a wide smile.

"No," I'm quick to say.

"Maybe later this week?" She is relentless—and not used to the word no in response to any of her questions. "Think about it, Jill. Will you?"

I shake my head and walk out the door, leaving her in the lobby. On the drive home, I try to make sense of what that was about. Maybe Ali is so complex, I won't ever be able to make sense of her. But she's not like her brother and her father. For all his faults, Jeffrey is always straightforward and direct. Sebastian is a schemer but I've always managed to read his plans right off his face. Ali's more complicated. I don't know what she wants. Or maybe I don't want to know. If what she really wants is to kiss me again, then I definitely don't want to know.

15

ALI

I'M IN WEST HOLLYWOOD, at a party at the Mondrian, and, as my gaze skims the blue surface of the pool, I'm reminded of Jill's eyes. They're the color of a pool—the same unnaturally bright blue.

Since Jill didn't want to have dinner with me, I decided to come here for my daily dose of evening entertainment. Asking her was a spur-of-the-moment decision—going to her office and trying to get under her skin wasn't. Ever since Madison uttered the thought that, perhaps, Jill might have enjoyed being kissed by me, I haven't been able to get the idea out of my head. Earlier, she certainly didn't act as though she wanted it to happen again, but if there's one thing Jill must have gotten used to over all the years of working for my father, it must be hiding her true feelings.

I sip from my cocktail. I don't even know what it is. Someone thrust it into my hand earlier and maybe these days it's unsafe to drink whatever you're given, but I don't much care.

Even though I've been away, and most of the people here are at least five, if not ten years younger than me, it feels as if I know at least half of them. Or they're pretending to know me. That's what I liked about being abroad. The name Lennox didn't mean anything there and it didn't come with any expectations. All I got asked was if I was related to Annie, to which I always replied, "I wish."

"Ali?" A woman has sidled up to me, pushing into the circle I'm physically part of, but to which I'm not contributing anything conversationally.

"Who's asking?" I manage to pull my lips into a smile.

"Hi, I'm Virginia."

"Ouch," I say. "What was it like going to high school with that name?"

"Exactly as you'd imagine." Virginia smiles back at me and pushes her bangs out of her eyes.

The circle of acquaintances seems to disperse a little, as though everyone's in on something I'm not, and they've decided to give me privacy. I don't mind at all because, despite her name, Virginia is absolutely ravishing to look at. And she's only wearing a skimpy bikini.

"Good line," I say, amping up the smile. "Do you always go up to girls calling them Ali?"

"Only you." Virginia fixes her gaze on me and holds it.

It could be this easy, I think. Pity I'm not much of a fan of easy.

"What do you do, Virginia?" I can't help but put some emphasis on her name.

"Sound effects." Only in L.A. can you say something like that and have it completely understood.

"Been working on anything fun of late?"

"We do a lot of action movies. Bullets and the screeching of tires and stuff like that. *The Hard Man* franchise and the likes."

"*The Hard Man* franchise?" I've genuinely never heard of it.

"Just another derivative, misogynistic, very successful Hollywood product." She puts her hands on her waist, dragging my gaze to her taut belly. "I love that you've never seen a *Hard Man* movie."

"Well, it does sound kind of porn-y and hard men aren't really my jam, either way."

"I get it. You're L.A.'s most eligible lesbian." Virginia's smile has turned into a seductive grin.

I have to chuckle. "Is that so? I'm hardly the only lesbian heiress in Hollywood."

"Of course not. Some of them even introduce themselves with the title 'heiress.'"

"As though it's an actual accomplishment to be born in a family with money."

"You're different. I can tell," Virginia says.

Ah, the forwardness of L.A. girls. Having traveled all over, and having been chatted up by people from all walks of life and all areas of the world, none of them have ever displayed the easy confidence of Americans, and especially SoCal women who look like Virginia. Being a quintessential L.A. girl myself, I can relate to her.

"How can you tell?" I put my empty glass on a nearby table.

"You don't walk into a place as if you own it."

"I don't own the Mondrian." In fact, I think, I'm getting a little too old to hang out by the Mondrian's pool on a Monday night.

"You know what I mean." Virginia suddenly looks coy.

I try to gauge her age. Her skin is smooth and there's not a wrinkle to be found on any patch of skin I can see—and I can see a lot—but in L.A. that doesn't really mean anything. "How old are you?" I might as well be direct as well.

"Ooh. That's a loaded question."

"Is it?" I arch up my eyebrows. "I'm thirty-five." I half-expect Virginia to run for the hills upon learning my age.

"The hell you are," she says.

A few minutes earlier, I was thinking this was easy, but this conversation is starting to annoy me. Then again, if I didn't want to get complimented on how I look younger than my age, I shouldn't have come here tonight. Maybe I shouldn't have come back to L.A. at all. But Daddy called; and I came. This reminds me of the question Jill asked me earlier about the relationship I have with my father. Because he's the only parent I've had for most of my life, a part of me does want his recognition. Maybe that's why I came back. I've never gotten much else from him, except, of course, the best care money can buy—as long as he didn't have to get involved himself.

"I'm twenty-six," Virginia says.

I've never had any qualms about taking home someone almost ten years younger than I am, but tonight, it doesn't seem to entice me very much. If anything, Virginia's youth puts me off. I'm not interested in what she has to offer, nor am I interested in being the kind of person I would pretend to be with her: easy, playful, carefree. I've pretended to be all of those for far too long. Now that I'm back, it shouldn't just be for business reasons. Maybe it's time to find out who I really am—and Virginia isn't going to help me increase the depth of knowledge that I need.

I let her down easy—another skill perfected over the years—and go home. After all, I have work tomorrow—and another chance to ask Jill out to dinner.

16

JILL

"How's Ali doing?" Jeffrey asks.

"Good." Much better than you, I think, when I scrutinize his face. The whites of his eyes are yellowish and his skin is gray. "How are *you*, Jeffrey?" I've always assumed if there was something seriously wrong with his health, I'd be the first to know. But I should really stop assuming.

"I have a very persistent chest infection." He coughs weakly, then waves off my question. "Can we fast-track her?"

"How fast are we talking?" My suspicions about his health flare up.

"I'd like to introduce her next month. Can you get her ready?"

"Next month?" I start pacing around his office. "Why so quickly? That's not what we agreed on."

"I know it's not, but I want to do it next month. All I need to know is if you can make it happen."

"It doesn't just depend on me, Jeffrey. Have you talked to Ali about this?"

"I wanted your opinion first."

"Next month is problematic, but that doesn't mean it can't

be done." In a way, this is good news for me. In fact, Ali could be introduced as Jeffrey's successor next week, it wouldn't make that much difference, because she has me. "Are you thinking of stepping down earlier than planned?"

He glares at me from behind his desk. "I might have no choice."

"What's really going on, Jeffrey?"

He just shakes his head. I will have to find out another way. There must be a reason he's not telling me. Or perhaps him asking me to fast-track Ali for the announcement is his way of telling me.

"I'll get it done. Don't worry."

He nods and I take it as my cue to leave.

When I'm back in my office, I call Ali. She'll have to rush through her tour of the departments. It's time for us to shift our plan into the next gear.

"Yes, Boss," she says, sounding very upbeat.

"I've decided to take you up on that offer for dinner this week," I say.

"Have you now?" Her tone has a triumphant note to it.

"Tonight would be good. We need to discuss business."

"You're on. How private does the conversation need to be?"

"As private as possible." I'm sure Ali knows the most private dining spot in Los Angeles.

"How about you come to my house?"

"Your house?" A red flag goes up immediately. "Next thing you'll tell me you'll cook for me."

"Uh, no, don't be silly, Jill. I'll get one of my father's chefs to come over."

"Can you ask them to come to my apartment instead?"

"Of course." She sounds as though I might regret my decision to invite her into my home again—but I need her to help me find out what's really going on with Jeffrey. She might not be very close to him, but she's his daughter.

"Your place it is," Ali says, as though she has just scored a major victory in a battle I'm somehow also a part of.

Ali arrives with four people in tow. Once we've set them up in the kitchen, I pull her aside and ask if we can trust them.

"That really depends on what your plans are, Jill," she says, sounding every bit the obnoxious brat she can be. But I've seen a different side of her and it's that side I focus on. I have no choice. At this time, in our brittle equation, I need her more than she needs me.

We take our drinks outside and I close the sliding doors to the patio.

"Have you spoken to your dad?"

"Not today," she says. "And not yesterday either, nor during the weekend. You'd think for a guy whose position I'm being groomed to take over, he'd keep me closer, but he doesn't. Have you?"

"He wants to announce you next month."

Ali keeps her composure. She does it better than most, but I notice the slight shift in her posture and the crease that briefly deepens between her eyebrows. "Why?"

"That's still a bit of a mystery to me. Do you know if his health has taken a sudden turn?"

Ali shakes her head. "I really don't know anything."

"It would be really good if we could find out."

"And by 'we' you mean 'me'?" I appreciate how things don't have to be spelled out for Ali.

"Yes."

"I'll try, but I'm not exactly my dad's confidante... I'll try Sebastian first. He may know more. And I can go by the house. If something's seriously wrong, the staff must know."

"Is he... seeing anyone at the moment?"

"Your guess is as good as mine."

"It's time to kick things into gear. I'm going to have to pull you from your rotation through the different departments and you're going to have to learn as you go along."

"But you still have my back." She locks her gaze on mine.

"We're doing this together. That's why you're here tonight."

A knock comes on the glass door. A guy dressed as a waiter slides it open.

"Would you like us to set the table outside?" he asks.

"That would be lovely." I send him a warm smile. "What's your name?"

"Neil," he says.

"Thanks, Neil."

Ali and I look over the balustrade, to the city below us, as our dinner table is being prepped.

"It feels quite extravagant to have four people in my home preparing dinner."

"You can't do it with less." Ali looks at me as though she knows very well that she's exaggerating. "One chef, one sous-chef, one sommelier, and a waiter."

"A sommelier?" I burst out laughing. "He couldn't have picked the wine beforehand?"

Ali shrugs. She's not used to occupying herself with such details. In that respect, she'll make a good CEO—as long as she does what I tell her.

I hold up my glass of, it needs to be said, excellent white wine. "To our partnership."

"Yeah." Ali sucks her bottom lip into her mouth and I swear she's looking at me the way she did just before she kissed me, even though the moment was so brief I barely remember it.

17

ALI

TALKING to Jill is light-years removed from being chatted up by Virginia last night. And not just because we have an already existing partnership to discuss.

We're halfway through dinner and I'd like to sit on Jill's deck forever, with the mountains in the background, dusk slowly settling around us.

"Are you nervous?" I ask. "About the whole CEO thing?"

"It will be a big change for me. I've been COO for quite a few years and Jeffrey has always been my boss."

"How much time between the announcement and me actually becoming CEO?"

"That depends on the board and on him, but I have to tell you, Ali, he really didn't look good this afternoon."

Maybe my father being unwell should make me feel all sorts of things, but it's hard to care for someone you barely know. For a lot of years, he's only been my father in name and by blood. After Mom died, he was always working. He's got one of the largest breweries in the world to show for it, but also a lousy relationship with his children. Even though Sebastian stayed around and that makes their rapport different, it's not any less complex.

"I'll get to the bottom of it." I don't feel like talking about my father or the company any longer. It's bad enough that I'll have to carve out some time to spend with my dad and Sebastian.

"Now that you've been back in L.A. for a while, are you happy you returned?" Jill asks.

"Very." I drop my cutlery and glance at her. "L.A. will always be my home. It's strange, you know? I lost so much here and I'm not close to what remains of my family, yet, there's something about this city that feels so profoundly like home."

"Your roots are here." Jill stops eating as well. "That was really delicious. Can you send these people over to my apartment again soon?" The light outside is getting sparse, but I can see the skin around her eyes crinkle when she smiles.

"Any time. It should be a company perk, really." I take another sip from the Sancerre the sommelier poured earlier. "Where are your roots? You're not from L.A. originally, are you?"

"I'm from the other coast. I grew up in upstate New York. Moved to the city as soon as I could. Went to NYU. Came out west more than twenty years ago."

"Did the Big Apple lose its crunch?"

Jill chuckles. "Many reasons, but a change of scenery was definitely one of them."

"Have you never wanted to return?"

"I go to New York often enough and I see my parents regularly."

"I mean, more permanently. Like I did, coming back to my roots."

Jill looks relaxed and as though she doesn't mind my probing questions too much.

"Not yet. And you can't beat the L.A. weather. I don't miss East Coast winters."

"No brothers and sisters or nieces and nephews that would like for you to live closer to them?"

"I'm an only child, so..."

"Don't you miss your New York friends?"

"Not anymore. And New York isn't that far away. I haven't moved to the other side of the world."

"Are you still in touch with people in New York?"

Jill takes a while to reply this time. "Not really. I left under... difficult circumstances. You might say I had to reinvent myself in L.A. And I did. If some of my former friends could see me now, they wouldn't believe their eyes."

"Why?" Even though Jill is sharing, there still something very reticent about her.

"I was a different person in New York. Much more, I don't know, naive and radical and foolish." She takes her glass of wine and looks into the distance.

"Sounds like how I was when I left L.A."

"Maybe, but your circumstances were very different, Ali." She turns to me and offers me a warm smile. "What was your favorite place on your tour abroad?"

"That's a tough one, because each city had its own particular charm. I loved Paris, even though I couldn't really do a lot of work there because my French isn't exactly fluent and the French *love* their French. And even when they spoke English, I could barely make out what they were saying." I pause. "I know my father hasn't always taken my time working abroad for Lennox seriously, but it was very serious to me. Yes, I partied, because what else was I going to do in the evenings? Sit at home and think about Leah and how she was no longer there and how everything would have been a million times better if she had been?"

I scan Jill's face for any signs of disapproval. I'm sure she's been thoroughly briefed on my accomplishments of the past decade—and all the targets I didn't meet. But she looks at me with an open gaze, no judgment in her glance at all. "Anyway, everyone always cut me a lot of slack because of what happened to Leah, and I did take advantage of that. And, well, my dad must have changed his mind about me at some point, otherwise he wouldn't have asked me to come back. Did he... ever talk about me to you?"

"Sometimes. Brief mentions. But it was enough that it was obvious you were in his thoughts. Jeffrey's so in his head, always thinking, always parsing the information that flows toward him non-stop, always trying to make the right decision. That's what he lives for. But that has changed recently, since before you came back. It's been one health scare after another. Never anything life-threatening, but it adds up. And I think it's a big blow for him that his body is letting him down more and more. That he's getting old. Maybe he somehow believed he was above that."

"Sounds like Dad." I appreciate her honest answer. "Have you been to Paris?"

Jill shakes her head. "Haven't had the opportunity."

"Do you want to go?"

"Sure. Some time. Maybe when I retire."

"Fuck retirement, Jill." Something inside me lifts—it always does when I have an idea like this. "Why wait until you're old like Dad? We can be in Paris this weekend if we want to. Say the word and I'll make it happen."

Jill shakes her head. "I don't doubt that you can do that, Ali. Not for one second. But I don't think so."

"Why not?" I'm like a dog with a bone now. "What's stopping you?"

"Let's see. Work, for starters. I always have things to catch up on Saturday. And I don't much feel like arriving at the office on Monday with jet lag. Also, the idea is just too outrageous. It's madness. It's something *you* would do."

"That doesn't make it something you couldn't do." I lean my

elbows on the table. "You can work on the flight, if you really have to. But ask yourself this, Jill: what will happen if you don't work for 48 hours? What's the absolute worst that can happen? You have a team, don't you? And you won't be dropping off the face of the planet. You'll be reachable—for emergencies only. And I promise you that if you take an actual weekend off, you'll return to work so much more refreshed on Monday. Plus, I have some tricks to beat jet lag. Sounds to me as though your arguments are not valid."

I can't help but smile smugly, although that's probably not the best course of action. I also need to take a minute to ask myself what the hell I'm doing asking Jill to go to Paris? But I've started this. I need to finish it now, otherwise it'll sit in my gut like a missed opportunity.

"You may have forgotten that we have to get you board-approved very soon. We should both be working overtime the next few weeks."

"Have you ever even heard of work-life balance, Jill? It's all the rage these days. I know my father doesn't practice it, but it's his company. It's different for him. And I bet he wishes that he'd been on more impromptu visits to Paris now."

"Ali, I'm not going to Paris with you this weekend. It's out of the question."

Jill's words are like a red rag to the bull inside of me. The more she protests, the more I want her to come.

"How about this: we'll be together all weekend long. You can update me on all the LB secrets for hours on end, with no one listening in or becoming suspicious. Look at it as an intense team building activity, because you and I, we're a team now, Jill."

18

JILL

I've gotten to know Ali well enough to know that I'm going to have to throw her a bone if I want her off my back at all for the rest of the evening. She has inherited her father's stubbornness. But whereas I can usually work with stubbornness, in Ali, I will have to find a way to mold it into the thoughtfulness that being the big boss of a large corporation requires.

"Let me think about it. Don't make any arrangements yet," I say.

She nods. "Okay. I will need a few days' notice. Money can make a lot of things happen in very little time, but there are limits."

"Let me sleep on it."

Neil slides open the patio door and collects our plates.

"Ready for dessert?" he asks.

"Sure," we both say, and he disappears into the house again.

"I wonder what the sommelier is doing right now," I say, to change the subject.

"Letting some dessert wine breathe," Ali says, in all seriousness.

I've traveled in her circles for a while now, but I didn't grow up like this. There will always be something inside of me wanting to push back against this ridiculous lavishness.

"If you need any more convincing, I can go on for a while," Ali says.

"I bet you can, but it's fine. Just let me sleep on it." I pick up my glass of wine again. "I've had a bit too much of this."

Ali nods, although I can tell she has to keep herself from sharing more of the greatness of Paris. And it was true what I said, I have always wanted to go, but I've simply never taken the time. By the time I was earning enough money to afford such a getaway, I was too busy making the money to enjoy it. I guess I still am. At least in that respect, she has a point.

But it's as though Ali is always trying to convince me to do one thing or another. It's as if she sees me and has the spark of an idea, but there's no filter to stop herself going with it. That may be how she has lived her life, but I most certainly haven't. On the other hand, I am definitely entitled to a number of vacation days I've never used. I take the requisite week in summer and another one around Thanksgiving to visit my parents, but that's it.

Ali's suggestions may come out of the blue, but the things she says do have merit. And more and more, even in the media I consume, I encounter articles about taking adequate time off and giving the brain time to recuperate. If I don't, I might end up like Jeffrey. On the other hand, however, I don't see how a weekend in Paris with Ali could ever be relaxing. I'd have to have my guard up all the time, and she'll want to drag me from one thing to the next and will probably end up introducing me to her millennial friends from her time there. The whole thing will be so exhausting.

Neil serves us dessert. It looks like a banana, but it's actually ice cream encased in a white chocolate banana shape. Once again, it's scrumptious, and it makes me wonder why I don't spoil myself more. Maybe I think I don't deserve it? Maybe I feel like I can always work a little harder. Maybe, the crippling anxiety that made me flee New York like a thief in the night is still, after all this time, a part of me?

Maybe going to Paris with Ali on a whim is exactly what I need to do. If only I can make it so that she doesn't perceive it as another thing she succeeded in making me do, something I complied to, something she can lord over me in the future, when our partnership goes into effect and I will need memories of standing up to her to fall back on.

I'll do as I promised. I'll sleep on it and if, by morning, I can swing it so that something about it feels like it's on my terms, I might just say yes.

"I've been wondering about something," Ali says, after we've finished dessert and are on our second glass of the wine the sommelier paired with it. I'm no lightweight when it comes to drinking, but because of my small stature, I've learned to sip instead of actually drinking—and most sips are just pretend sips. But in this setting, it's harder to do. So when Ali asks me the question, I don't see it coming because of the fuzziness in my head.

"Was Melissa your lover?" she asks.

"Aren't you quite the detective tonight?"

"It doesn't take a lot of detecting when one of the most prominent pictures in your living room is of a woman you used to know."

"She could just be a friend."

"She could. Just a wild guess, then."

"Yes, she was my partner, back in New York."

"Thanks for telling me," Ali says, as though I've told her the biggest secret in the world. Or maybe she's just trying to encourage me to say more. "Is she the reason you moved to L.A.?" She just can't help herself. She always has to push. Always needs one more answer.

"That's a story for another time." I look at my watch. It's almost midnight. "How about we call it a night?"

"Sure. You need to sleep on something." She winks at me, then pushes herself out of her chair. "I'll go check on the state of your kitchen."

She heads inside and I look at her empty chair. I can't even remember the last time I had an evening like this in my own home. A dinner for two on my patio. Most evenings, my mind's too preoccupied to come out here and appreciate the beauty of my surroundings. At least Ali has given me that.

19

ALI

"Let's make a deal," Jill says. "If you can find out more about your dad's health, I'll go to Paris with you."

"Are you giving me a deadline to accomplish this?"

"Yes. The last possible moment you can arrange the trip." Jill looks pretty pleased with herself. I'm not sure if she has set me an impossible task or not. I'll find out soon enough. Maybe it's difficult enough in her eyes for her to be sure that she won't have to come with me. I try to detect the tiniest indication from her that she wants to go, but I can't. This is not the version of Jill I sat across from last night. This is corporate, buttoned-up Jill, although she's not wearing a turtleneck today.

"Okay, leave it with me. I'll report back tonight." At least I don't have to suffer through the internships she arranged for me any longer.

"Good luck."

I walk into my office, which still feels so foreign, and try to come up with a plan of action. I already had one that I came up with on the ride home last night, but now I will have to accelerate it. The first step is to talk to my brother. Only now, I will have to find a way to stay cool and collected so he doesn't become suspicious—I'll have to find a way to restrain my enthusiasm at the prospect of a weekend in Paris with Jill.

I only manage to see Sebastian at lunch, which he orders to have in his office.

"Gluten, lactose, and taste-free," he says, when I sit across from him.

"Sounds delightful." First, I need to find out if Dad has told him about announcing his successor earlier. "What have you been up to?" It's an innocuous enough question.

"Why don't you just come out and ask me what you really want to know?" His hackles are already up. Great. "How much coke have I been snorting?"

"That's really not what I meant, Seb. I just want to know who you've been hanging out with, what you did over the weekend… stuff like that."

"Ah, you want to pretend we're friends."

"I don't need to pretend. You're my fucking brother." My swearing always seems to increase exponentially when I'm around him.

"Which doesn't automatically make me your friend."

"Sure. Fine. What am I then? Your acquaintance? Your co-worker?" I'll be your boss soon enough, you moody mother-fucker, I think.

"Maybe I can be someone you hang out with from time to time. You don't have to go to every party in this town, you know."

"I don't. And we're hanging out now, aren't we?"

"And then, when you throw your own party," Sebastian continues as if he hasn't heard me, "at your own fucking house, you don't even invite me."

"I didn't think it would be your scene. Sorry."

"You could have given me the opportunity to turn down your invitation and let me be the judge of that."

"Fine. Next time, you're *numero uno* on my guest list. How did you know I had a party, anyway?"

"I make it my business to know everything that goes on in this family."

I wonder if he knows about my dinner at Jill's last night. I make a mental note to be more discreet.

"So what is going on in this family?" He's just handed me the perfect opening.

"You're being prepped for the big announcement."

I wait to see if he'll continue of his own volition, but he doesn't. It looks as though me being appointed CEO still doesn't sit very well with him.

"That's it?"

"Our family's quite small," he says on a sigh.

"How's Dad?" I ask.

"Dad's... Dad."

"You spend much more time with him than I do—"

"Yeah, about that," he cuts me off. "Just coming back might seem good enough for you, but it's not for the old man, okay? You should really spend some time with him."

"Wow, now I should spend time with both my brother and my father, neither of whom have ever given any indication that's what they want."

"You may think the only reason Dad asked you to come back is to be the face of the company for a while, but, you know, these days family seems to be more important to him. I swear the other day he wanted to talk about grandchildren, but I quickly disabused him of the notion that I would provide any. Unless you have any plans in that direction?" He smirks, as though it would hurt him to actually smile.

I'm trying to process all the information Sebastian is hurtling at me. My dad wants to spend time with me?

"Maybe we can get together some time soon."

"We should," Sebastian says. "How about this weekend? Or are you throwing another party?"

"This weekend might not work for me. I'm thinking about going away."

"Where? He sold Napa, so don't think about going there."

"Napa's sold?"

"Nobody had gone there in years."

"But Napa was always there." Leah always claimed that Dad only bought the vineyard to look more sophisticated—to not just be a beer man.

"Now it's not."

"Who bought it?"

"I really couldn't tell you." Sebastian finally starts picking at his food.

"I'm not sure yet where I'll go." It's true, because if Jill doesn't want to go to Paris, I'm not certain I'll want to go on my own. "I just want to get out of the city for a few days."

"It's probably too short notice for Dad, anyway," he says sullenly.

"Do you speak to his doctors?" I decide to forego the cardboard-looking lunch being offered to me altogether.

"No. Only Dad speaks to his doctors."

"Have you ever asked him about his health?"

"Are you out of your mind?"

"No, I don't believe I am. He's our father. We should know what's going on with him."

"You ask him then, Ali. See what he has to say to you about it."

I will do just that, I think. This conversation hasn't been very enlightening with regards to my father's health, so I can only get the information I need straight from the horse's mouth.

I walk up to Evelyn's office and ask for the first available appointment in my father's schedule.

"I'll see if he can squeeze you in now, Ali," she says, with a wink, and gently knocks on the door. She closes it behind her when she goes in, and comes out a few seconds later.

"You're in luck. Go on in."

I try to imitate the gentleness with which Evelyn opened the door, assuming that's how Dad likes his office door to be opened, but being brusque by nature I end up barging in as usual—I got my brusqueness from my Dad, so I'm sure he won't mind too much.

"Alexandra," he says, and smiles at me.

"Hi, Daddy."

"Has Jill talked to you?" He cuts right to the chase. Maybe I truly only have a few seconds to have this conversation.

"About moving up the announcement date?" I sit as close to him as possible so that I can observe his features. Jill was right, he does look a bit worse for wear. "Yes, she has. We're working on it."

What strikes me most of all is that he no longer looks like the formidable man I used to be scared of—all three of us were. His shoulders are slightly hunched forward and, at times, he looks as though he is gasping for breath. He's just a shadow of the man I left behind ten years ago. Maybe that's what losing Leah did to him, over time.

"Is there a reason why we're speeding things up?" In this moment, he looks pliable enough to give me a straight answer.

"Of course there's a reason." The thunder has returned to his voice briefly.

"Do you want to share that reason with me?"

He sighs. "I do, but I'm not sure I can. Not right now. Maybe you should come to the house. You and Sebastian." Christ, he and my brother really are beating the same drum—for different reasons, I imagine.

"Of course, Daddy. Whenever you want." I just hope he doesn't say this weekend.

"Come tonight."

"Tonight?" It's not often my father has an evening off to spend with his children. "Sure."

"Tell Evelyn on your way out, will you? Tell her to call the house etcetera."

"Okay." Is this my cue to leave? He doesn't say any more and returns his attention to the stack of papers in front of him.

I get up and head to the door.

"Alex—Ali," he says, suddenly. But he doesn't say anything else, despite me getting the distinct impression he wants to. "I'll see you tonight. Let's say eight."

20

JILL

"I'M GOING to the house tonight," Ali says, as though I should be packing my bags for Paris already. "Dinner with Dad and Sebastian."

"Good." Even though Ali's none the wiser yet, I'm still impressed by the progress she has made.

"And you were right. He doesn't look as though his health is very good."

"If you need to talk afterward, call me," I say, without thinking.

"Sure. I'll let you know what I've found out."

"I don't just mean that, Ali. If your father gives you bad news and you need to process, you can always call me for that as well," I say.

"Everyone's really going soft around here these days," she jokes. "So I might as well hold you to that and do the same."

"Don't tell them about Paris."

"I won't. It's not even certain we're going yet, or is it?"

"No, it's not." I do feel a twinge of guilt—this is her father's health I'm bargaining with here. "Look." Once again, I feel the need to give in, to accommodate her in some way. It's not a sensation I experience with anyone else. Ali is the perfect blend of the boss's daughter and the girl with no mother who also lost her twin sister. I can't help but extend kindness after kindness to her, even if that translates sometimes into submitting to her silly whims. "If we don't make it this weekend, I'm sure another time will be convenient." I'm basically saying that I want to go to Paris with her, which does take me aback a bit. But she has gotten under my skin—and that dinner last night was highly pleasant. And it's good that we're becoming friends. I'd rather work closely with someone I consider a friend than someone who will always keep me at arm's length, like Jeffrey. Sebastian is something else altogether—and I've never considered him my boss, although, in some ways, he is.

"Good," Ali says. "You're fifty-three and you haven't been to Paris. How is that even possible?"

"I've been busy." I've had to work to acquire money, I think. This will always be the most fundamental difference between us. Ali has worked for Lennox Breweries for more than ten years now, but I doubt her salary pays for much of her lifestyle. Thank goodness for trust funds. And when you're a Lennox child, 'work' seems to be quite a stretchable term.

"I know, Jill. I was only teasing."

"I have to get back to *work* now, Ali."

She nods. "I'll call you tonight, without a doubt," she says and heads out the door.

The second she's gone, Linda walks in, like she's been waiting at the door. I hope she hasn't been listening, although I do trust Linda. Still, some pieces of information, like the state of the CEO's health, have a tendency to spread like wildfire.

"Any progress with Ali?" she asks.

"She's doing well." I wouldn't normally be so vague with Linda, but what can I possibly tell her? She made me go to one of her parties and tried to kiss me? I do, however, realize that Linda's as close to a confidante as I have. Still, I'm not telling her anything. It's more a reflection on the state of my personal life and the lack of friendships in it. I learned to live with that once I made the decision that Lennox Breweries would be part of my legacy, despite not being born a Lennox.

"Does she talk about Leah?" Linda's been with Lennox even longer than me.

"Sometimes. I get the impression that..." That what? That the worst of her pain is over? I can't make a claim like that about another person. "Let's just say that being away has been good for her."

"Poor thing," Linda says. "To lose her mother at such a young age and then her sister."

The same can be said for Sebastian, of course, yet we've worked with him for too long to still feel sorry for him. Ali's presence is still fresh, bringing with it the memories of when it happened. Jeffrey only missed one day of work—the day of the funeral. The evening before, his face as stoic as ever, he told me he'd be available by phone if something urgent came up, as though I wouldn't be attending the funeral.

"Human beings are resilient," I say. Maybe this stopped applying to Jeffrey, however. He was already in his seventies when Leah died, although you wouldn't have thought him older than in his early sixties. After her death, although he did his very best to work so hard—maybe so that he wouldn't feel the worst of the pain—ever so slowly, his health started to suffer. It could simply be old age, but considering his family history, it might be more than that.

"Does she have a girlfriend?"

I don't know why this question makes my cheeks warm up. "Not that I know of."

"She probably has a few. She's a catch. She'll probably snag some Hollywood starlet. It's all the rage for them to be going out with women these days—especially if they can be snapped by some paparazzo." Linda stands there smiling.

We never discuss my sexual preference or my dating life, yet I take offense. But I'm still not the kind of person to voice my annoyance about this.

"Was there something you wanted, Linda?" My voice does sound a bit sharp. Maybe because my heart shrank a bit at the thought of Ali with a gorgeous actress on her arm, walking some red carpet, smiling into the camera.

"I need you to look at this research."

I shift into work mode, which, I also realize, was much easier to do before Ali returned.

21

ALI

SEBASTIAN and I have been at the house for half an hour before Dad arrives. We've been nursing drinks and, the more of that we've done, the wilder our speculations of what our father is about to tell us have become. Because he must have some sort of announcement to make—we wouldn't be here if he didn't.

When he joins us in the sitting room, Janine, the housekeeper, doesn't even offer him a choice of beverage. She just pours him a glass of mineral water with a wedge of lime.

"I'm not going to make you wait for it," Dad says. "I always thought it was bullshit, or that I was immune to it, but apparently, stress isn't very good for the health of your cardiovascular system." He sits in the same chair he's been sitting in since Mom was alive. It gets newly upholstered every year. The latest fabric is burgundy red and it makes Dad's skin look even grayer. "Long story short, I'm going to need bypass surgery sometime soon, after Ali has been announced as my successor."

"What?" Sebastian jumps up. "Oh shit." He starts pacing.

"It's fine, Son." Dad makes a tempering gesture with his hand.

"When did the doctor tell you that you need surgery?" I ask.

"Yesterday." He locks his eyes on me, his gaze much softer than any time I remember.

"Is it recommended that you wait?" I hold his gaze.

Dad just shrugs. "It doesn't matter. I can't have surgery now. We need to announce you as the next CEO first. You understand that."

"Of course, Dad," Sebastian says.

"No fucking way." I jump out of my chair as well. "Your health is more important than the Lennox share price."

"Maybe you don't understand." My dad's gaze has long slipped away from me.

"I do. I understand perfectly. In fact, I think I'm the only one who does." I glare at Sebastian. I'm not sure this is a fight I can win on my own.

"Ali, calm down," Sebastian says. "Dad knows what he's doing."

"I want to speak to your doctor. Now." I pick up my father's phone from the table next to him, even though I have no clue as to his cardiologist's name. One thing I am sure of, however, is that when he sees it's Jeffrey Lennox calling, he'll pick up. "Call him, Dad." I hand him the phone, which he drops back onto the table.

"You can talk to him tomorrow, Ali."

"You're only planning to announce at the end of the month. Surely it's not safe to wait that long."

"I take hypertension medication and all my vitals are monitored twice a day," Dad says. "I'm not going to keel over and die, Ali."

"You probably shouldn't even be in the office. For fuck's sake." Anger rises in me. It sits in my stomach like bile. Am I really the only one who's worried about another death in the family? I make eyes at Sebastian again to urge him to help me talk some sense into our father.

"I work from home sometimes," Dad says feebly. He doesn't

even seem to have the vim to fight me on this. It's as though he made the decision and he'd rather—literally—die than not stick to it. That sounds like the father I know.

"You're not waiting to have this surgery, Dad. That's just crazy. If you die, what will it matter if the share price drops?" Someone has to say the d-word, and it looks like it won't be Sebastian.

"It matters for you. And for the company that I've built. It's not going down with me."

"It won't." I want to say something else indelicate, but I should probably wait until Dad has digested my previous remark.

"Ali, you've only just come back," Sebastian chimes in. "It would be very bad optics if Dad were to go into hospital all of a sudden to have bypass surgery."

"No one has to know it's heart surgery. Surely we can buy some discretion."

"Ali, you're not listening. I'm not having surgery before my successor has been announced and stability for the company is ensured. It's not just the optics. I'm not going under, with the risk of never waking up again, without this being resolved." He's out of breath already.

"That's easy then. Resolve it. Announce me tomorrow."

"I would if I could, but you've only just returned. How will that look?"

"I get that it's time you need, but time is what you don't have, Dad." He's right to question my competence, of course. I'm not ready to lead the brewery. But I know someone who is. "Why don't you make Jill interim CEO?"

Sebastian scoffs.

I turn to him. "Why not?"

"She's not family," he says, as though that's the most important trait needed to become the big boss.

"She's the absolute best person for the job. She knows

everything. She's been with the company for over twenty years. She's mentoring me to become CEO. I'll be the first to admit that I'm not ready. But she is."

"I need to think about it," Dad says.

Janine walks into the sitting room. "Dinner's served," she says.

"You kids may want to get something else other than the rabbit food that's been prepared for me," Dad says.

I look at Sebastian to help me ascertain if we should take this as our cue to leave, but he follows Dad into the dining room, and so do I.

22

JILL

It's way past ten o'clock when Ali finally calls me.

"Where are you?" is the first thing she asks.

I had expected her voice to sound all triumphant and smug with the knowledge she gathered to lure me to Paris but she sounds small—like I've never heard her before

"In my apartment," I reply.

"Can I come over?"

"Of course. Ali, are you okay?"

"I'd rather tell you in person," she says, then goes silent.

"Of course. Come on over. I'll be waiting."

While I wait for Ali, I prepare for the worst. It doesn't take someone with a medical degree to see that Jeffrey hasn't been well. Maybe it's worse than I allowed myself to imagine. All the possibilities show up as an endless slew of lit-up words in my mind: cancer, heart disease, Alzheimer's, cancer again. He's not a young man and the untimely death of his daughter, added to the high-pressured environment he chooses to immerse himself in every single day, must have taken a toll.

Ali barges in, her eyes a little red, but not bloodshot enough for me ask if she's been crying.

"It's heart disease. He needs bypass surgery," she says. "Do you have his doctor's phone number? I would really like to call him."

"Ali." I put my hands on her shoulders. "Calm down. It's late. We can't be calling anyone now."

"He's a doctor and this is a fucking emergency, Jill."

"Talk to me." I coax her to the couch and sit her down.

"He won't have the surgery until he has announced the new face of the company, but I'm not ready. Not for the board to accept me, let alone the shareholders. Why did I stay away so long? I should have been here. I should have seen this happening. Why didn't anyone fucking tell me?"

It suddenly seems to be hitting Ali hard that she might lose another member of her family. I don't think she even knew herself how much she cared about her father before now. "Ali. Darling." I put my hand in the back of her neck. "This is not your fault. Your father is a very stubborn man. He was always going to wait until the last possible moment to confide in you."

"He shouldn't have had to confide in me. I should have noticed. It was so obvious tonight that he's seriously ill."

"Then we'll do everything we can to make him better."

She finally looks at me. Her eyes are a little moist. "I told him to have the surgery as soon as possible and to appoint you as interim CEO."

My eyebrows arch up of their own accord.

"It makes perfect sense. Even I can see that," Ali says. "Dad said he needed to think about it, but surely he must have thought about it before."

I let a short silence fall as I process Ali's words. What she's proposing isn't too far removed from what we had initially planned. "What did Sebastian say?"

"He didn't agree because you're not family, but that's bullshit. Besides, who else is going to do it? Him?"

"Your dad doesn't want him."

"My dad... might be gone soon." Her voice cracks a little.

"He has the best care money can buy." It sounds so hollow—so inadequate.

Ali shakes her head. "If that's the case, why isn't his doctor insisting he have the surgery straight away? On the way over, I did some research. This is not a surgery to hold off on, Jill. He's doing it for the company. For fucking Lennox Breweries, which is the very reason we never saw him after Mom died. And now he's going to let it kill him."

"It's his life's work."

"And Sebastian and I are his children. What's more important?"

"Different things are important to different people." I haven't had a conversation this emotionally charged in a very long time.

"At least I know where I stand now."

"I'll talk to him." Not that it will do much good.

"You can't tell him that you know about this. This sort of thing needs to stay under wraps. He won't like me blabbing to you."

"I know." Over the years, I've become an expert on Jeffrey Lennox as well. "He'll have to tell me eventually."

"But eventually might be too late. I want him to have the operation this week." She shoots me a sideways glance. "I won't be able to take you to Paris."

"Forget Paris, Ali."

"You can go on your own."

That sounds about as appealing as the prospect of having heart surgery. "Forget it," I repeat. "It could be that he's scared, you know."

"My dad?" Ali scoffs. "I've never known him to be scared of anything."

"He was scared when you left... He's scared for Sebastian and the addiction he can't seem to kick."

"Scared is not the word I would use. Perhaps he harbors a small amount of concern."

"He lost his wife when she was only—" To my shame, I don't remember how old Veronica was.

"Mom was thirty-four when she died. One year younger than I am now," Ali says.

Then it dawns on me that who is most scared of all is this woman sitting next to me, who has lost so much already.

"Maybe we're all a little scared." I curve my arm all the way around her shoulders.

"I'm scared. I mean, to be completely honest, Jill, some days I don't even know if I want to be CEO. What kind of life is that, anyway? I've seen what it's done to my dad. He was never there. Not even when we needed him most of all. If that's the kind of person this job turns you into, then I might actually want to pass. Sebastian can have it." She shudders as she inhales deeply. Then she leans her head on my shoulder. "I really don't care about Lennox Breweries *that* much."

"You're upset," I whisper in her ear. "You need a good night's sleep. Maybe a night cap."

"Will you join me?" Her heads tilts toward me.

"Of course. What can I get you?" I know I have to move—remove myself. This is beginning to look a lot like that time in her bedroom. But I seem to be physically incapable of doing so, of even putting one more inch between us.

"I'll have this," she says, and closes her eyes. Then, she kisses me.

And I let her.

This time, I don't care about decorum or how preposterous it is. I kiss her right back. Her lips open slightly as I press mine against hers. She turns her head, then her body, so she faces me. There's a small distance between us and I'm the one who bridges it. I cup her chin in my hands and draw her near. I don't need to check in with some hidden part of myself. I don't need permission from anyone, least of all myself—I would never give myself permission if I were to ask, anyway. I surrender wholly and completely to what I feel in that moment, and my single-most desire is to feel Ali's lips against mine again.

Her eyes flutter open and shut and then they disappear from my field of vision because I'm kissing her again. Her tongue meets mine and the contact sets all of my skin on fire. It awakens something inside of me that I haven't allowed myself to feel for years. And why? Perhaps, if I hadn't denied myself the occasional bout of passion—love, even—I wouldn't be kissing the boss's daughter right now. But Ali has ceased to be Jeffrey Lennox's daughter. She has to. She's my friend. A woman I've gotten to know better and, who, just by being herself, has gotten under my skin. Where her foolish actions and words used to infuriate me, they now awaken something else entirely.

"You're not pulling back," she says, when we break for some much-needed air.

"I'm not," I state the obvious.

"Why?" She's slightly breathless.

"Because I don't want to."

"Is this… okay now?"

I shrug. "I really don't know. But how could it be wrong?" In many, many ways, flashes through my mind. Ali's vulnerable tonight. Am I taking advantage of that? She will still be my boss at some point. Jeffrey would fire me if he found out. But I look into Ali's eyes, not a hint of brazenness in them, and I know none of that matters. Not right now. She needs someone. She needs more than words. She needs someone who cares, and I do.

23

ALI

I DID IT AGAIN. I kissed Jill again. I didn't mean to. I certainly didn't come here with that intention in mind. I just did it. A wave of desire came over me and I pressed my lips to hers and, this time, she didn't pull back. This time, she kissed me back. And her question lingers between us: how could it be wrong?

It will always be a little bit wrong—that's probably one of the reasons why, since I've met her, I've wanted to kiss her so badly. But the reasons are of no importance now. Because in that sense, Jill is correct. How could this be wrong when it feels so incredibly good—so utterly right?

I lean in again and, as I do, I marvel at the shape of her lips, at the wonder of them. They look as though their sole purpose in life is to be kissed and to kiss back. And Jill's kiss is divine. It sucks me right in, tethers me to her, makes me never want to leave this place, her couch, her arms. A hot flash courses through me, and it hits me that, when it comes to Jill Gold, I want so much more than this kiss. First of all, I want to know so much more about her. I want to know who the woman in the picture is. I want to know why she works so much. I want to know what she looks like underneath that turtleneck sweater. Is she hiding something?

"Oh, fuck, Ali," she says, on a sigh, when our lips part. "What are we doing?"

For the first time, I seem to lose all my game around her. Because I have been playing her. From the very beginning, I've been testing her boundaries. And I haven't always been nice to her and I've made her do things she didn't want to do. All the while, she has shown me such kindness, which is not something I always respond to, but with her, I do.

"The fuck if I know." My breath comes quickly. God, I want her. I don't know if I can have her—I don't know if I should.

"I want… more," she says, "but I'm not sure it's a good idea."

"Even if it was the worst idea in history, it still wouldn't matter." I look into her steel-blue eyes. "We both know that." It seems like my game is back. I wish it wasn't. I wish I could just stop and just be me. Show my true self. Hasn't Jill shown me enough that I can trust her?

"Do you want that drink now?" she asks.

"Jill," I whisper. "I only want you." And what I'm saying—it comes from the bottom of my heart. I bring my hand to her cheek and caress her skin with the back of my fingers. "Do you want me?"

"Ali," she says, as though just saying my name is causing her pain. Then she nods.

Jill wants me. I try to parse the information, but my attention is already drawn to her pillowy lips again. She pursed them slightly when she nodded and it's an image I will never forget.

I kiss her again and, this time, it's different. The intention behind it is different. I know where it will take me. I don't know the details, but the outcome is secure, of that I'm sure as her lips touch mine.

And kissing Jill is different than kissing anyone else I've

ever kissed before. Because of the circumstance and because of who she is. She's not some girl I just met at a party. She's not someone I will want to kick out of my bed as soon as I'm done with her, although I can't be sure that she won't want to do that to me. It's also the challenge of that: of making sure Jill still wants me after tonight.

"Come with me," Jill whispers. Her lips look deliciously swollen. Her hair is disheveled even though I haven't touched it yet. She must be hot in that sweater. She takes my hand and leads me to her bedroom.

Once inside, she pulls me to her and I finally feel her entire body pressed against me. Because we're standing, I need to lean down considerably as she's so much shorter than me. I guide her toward the bed while our lips keep meeting clumsily.

"Wait," she says, before we lie down, and hoists her sweater over her head.

Finally.

Underneath, she's only wearing a bra—black as well. She kicks off her shoes and, all the while, she keeps her eager gaze on me. Of all the things I had expected to happen tonight, frantically getting rid of my clothes in Jill's bedroom wasn't one of them. I might have dreamed of it, after that first, stolen kiss, for a split second once in a while, but if I did, I relegated that thought to the back of my mind immediately. But perhaps this is what happens with thoughts like that when you try to ignore them. They come bursting to the fore with such undeniable force later.

My top has buttons that need to be undone and I'm much slower to undress than Jill. She's already on the bed in nothing but her underwear. When it hits me that this is actually Jill Gold sitting in front of me like that, I suddenly seem incapable of undoing any more of my blouse buttons. My fingers freeze at the sight of her, at the vulnerability of her near-naked body, at how ready she is for this.

Her gaze locks on mine again and she scoots to the edge to give me a hand. Although it's not really helping because she has put one hand on my belly and her touch ignites every nerve ending in my body. But it does spur me on to get at least as naked as she is. I let go of my aspirations to be all suave and cool in this moment. The only thing that matters is that Jill is waiting for me. She wants me. She said it—nodded it—earlier and it couldn't be more obvious now.

When I've finally stripped down to my underwear, which I just want to rip off as well, I join her on the bed. We stretch out and then, we're face-to-face again.

I look into her eyes and I forget about everything that has brought me here tonight. I only focus on her. On the two freckles on the right side of her nose. On the web of crows' feet circling her eyes. On those soft lips that I've now had the extended privilege of tasting. I already know that Jill Gold is a remarkable woman. She's smart and kind and tough when she needs to be. And I want her for all of those reasons.

She runs a finger along my side. "You're so gorgeous," she says.

"So are you," I reply, and I mean it. Because, in her own way, Jill is so much more beautiful than the last person I ended up in bed with. Or any actress or model I've been with and who would be considered objectively more beautiful than most people. And yet, to me, Jill Gold is the most beautiful woman I've ever had the privilege of seeing undressed, of running a finger over the skin of her belly, of losing myself in the dreamy blue pools of her eyes before I lean in to kiss her. And this time, another dimension is added again, because we're both almost naked and Jill's skin is warm and inviting and I just want to wrap myself around her and kiss her all night long.

So I throw my arms around her and hug her even tighter while I explore more of her lips and her tongue and then her neck and clavicle, where I would, one day, like to remain for an extended period of time. I taste her skin and inhale her scent until we reach that moment where we can't get any closer, any more intimate, without taking off the rest of our clothes.

She comes for my bra first, unhooks it with a steady hand. I lower it off my body and I watch her as her gaze is glued to my breasts. Her eyes widen a bit, as though she's truly in awe of what she's seeing—and maybe she is. Or maybe she's not. We have lots to talk about, but not right now. Because right now, I'm reaching behind her back and doing the same thing she just did to my bra, but once I've unhooked it, she doesn't remove it straight away. She presses her hands against the cups.

"I'm not… in my thirties. Or forties," she says, suddenly shy.

"You're beautiful," I repeat, and put a hand over hers.

"I don't look anything like you." This must be Jill at her most vulnerable.

"Thank goodness for that." I caress her hand, gently coaxing it away from the bra she's still holding up. It's all I can do, because this is not the time or place to give a speech about the complete unimportance of the tautness of her skin or the pertness of her breasts. I've been with plenty of women whose breasts were modeled and manipulated into something nature didn't intend them to be and not once has it given me the slightest shiver of pleasure to clasp my eyes on them. The greatest thing about Jill is that she's real. Everything about her is unfiltered. She still has plenty of East Coast in her and I bet she's never considered seeing a plastic surgeon.

Together, we remove her bra and, once it's gone, the need to cover herself seems to have disappeared with it. There's a new audacity in her glance, as though getting rid of the fabric covering her breasts has given her fresh confidence.

I can't help but reach for her. I cup her breast in my hand and I marvel at its warm softness. It feels so good in my hand, so perfect, so final, in a way. As though I'll never need to feel any other woman's breast again. This is it. I've come home in more ways than one.

I push her gently onto her back and lower myself on to her. I suck her nipple between my lips and then, the biggest marvel of all, she lets out a very gentle but extremely arousing little groan. Then she says my name.

"Oh, Ali," she moans, and it drives me completely crazy.

I shower her breasts with kisses and I taunt her nipples with my teeth. Jill squirms beneath me, until there's only one road left for me to take. I kiss her nipples one last time before making my way down. Jill doesn't seem to have any issues with taking off her panties. She pushes them down for me and I guide them off her legs and then she's naked in front of me.

24

JILL

I TAKE IN THE SIGHT. Ali's sitting on her knees. I can't keep my eyes off her breasts. No wonder I had a moment of hesitation when I took off my bra. She has the most sensational breasts I've ever seen. And she has also just taken off the last of my underwear. I would be lying if I claimed this isn't a bit of a mind-fuck. This is not why I told her she could come over. Yes, I wanted to comfort her, but this was not on my mind. Not even an inkling of it. And now look at me.

Ali leans over me again and she brings her face close to mine. I take the opportunity to—finally—roam my hands over her breasts, to catch her nipples between my fingers. Oh God. I'm about to combust with sheer arousal. And I don't know if it's her youthfulness that excites me so much, or her brazenness, or simply who she is. It's probably a little bit of everything. All I know for absolute certain in this moment is that I want her to fuck me. I want her hands all over me, inside me, giving me a release I didn't know I so sorely needed.

I need it more than I need to hold on to the last shred of my sanity. I pull her close to me, find her ear, and whisper, "I need you to fuck me now." Words I'd never thought I'd speak to anyone again. Not after Melissa. Even though I've been with other women since her, I've never asked this of them in that particular way. Merely saying the words sparks a new fire beneath my skin, as though it lights up at her touch, at the prospect of what's to come.

Ali looks down at me and nods gravely. She doesn't say anything. She looks almost solemn, as though I've just given her a very difficult task. Maybe I've overwhelmed her, but I really don't think so. Ali Lennox is more than up to it. Then the left corner of her mouth draws upward ever so slightly and she's herself again, the gravity of the moment has passed, and I know I'm in for the ride of my life. Because ever since that night in her room, something's been going on between us. I might have scolded her for kissing me at the time, but, deep down, that wasn't what I wanted to do. Now, I finally get to kiss her back, again and again. So I do. I pull her close and I kiss her deeply, while pressing her body against mine. Until she starts kissing my breasts again—she kisses them like they're the most beautiful breasts she's ever kissed. She takes away the last of my worries, because it's simply not possible to feel insecure when someone kisses you with such vigor.

Her kisses meander down and I spread my legs for her, and open to her fully. Then I welcome her—her hot breath at the apex of my thighs, her fingertips digging into my flesh, the increased heat of her actions.

Even the mattress feels different beneath me. I've slept in this bed a thousand times, yet it seems to yield more generously underneath me—underneath us.

Ali positions herself between my legs. Even though it's moments away from happening—it is, in fact, already happening—I still can't believe it. My sanity must have gone out of the window quite some time ago, because this is utter madness.

Then she pitches forward and it's not just her breath I feel.

She kisses me lightly on the thigh and my breath stalls in my throat. Her kisses keep landing on my inner thigh, as though she's painting some kind of pattern there, but if she is, it isn't one I can discern. I only feel the heat building between my legs, as though Ali's already firmly kissing me there. On my raging, pulsing clit. On that spot at the center of me that hasn't felt this alive in years. As a result, everything that's been dormant inside of me for far too long comes alive as well. I'm hyper-aware of the sounds in the room, of where Ali's hands are, of the small, soft moans that emanate from her mouth as she kisses me again and again. And then, her lips land on my clit and I'm the one who does all the moaning.

A long, loud yelp escapes me, as though that particular part of my body has been deprived for too long. And maybe it has, even though I hardly ever take the time to consider this. But it's something else as well, because, for the life of me, I can't remember any of the women I've been with in the past few years eliciting such a reaction from me. It's because it's Ali Lennox doing this to me, with all her pain and confidence and contradictions. It's because my subconscious already knows that this will be the one and only time this can happen. There are no encores. There's only tonight.

Her tongue flicks around my clit and with every touch, I lose more of my mind. This is the single-most arousing moment of my life since I met Melissa. Then it hits me that Ali reminds me of her, not in looks, because Melissa was all dark hair and heavy brows and eyes the color of summer grass. Ali looks very different, but her personality reminds me of Melissa. Maybe that's why I went to her stupid party that night. Maybe a part of me knew that if I didn't go, I'd miss out on something important.

Her fingertips dig deep into the flesh of my thighs and maybe it's foolish to see this as an effort, nevertheless, this is the most effort Ali has shown. The most devotion. The most passion. And I can't see her face but I see enough of her to know that she's all in, that she can be all in to something that's not solely centered around herself. To give someone else this kind of pleasure. To gently seduce them into allowing it is, for her, a selfless act. And isn't that exactly what she has done to me?

I'm not sure how much more of this I can take. My muscles tense up, the fire raging inside me spreads to every cell, Ali has turned me on to such an extent that I have no choice but to spur her on.

I bring a hand to her head to get her attention.

She smiles up at me from between my legs and the sight of her, the sparkle in her eyes, is enough to make me forget my most acute intention.

And then she just nods. She has understood. And, that, perhaps, is what floors me the most. To not have to say something out loud to someone, to have them wordlessly understand what you need, is a form of intimacy I've only ever once reached—because I've only ever let one person in like that. It's probably just a coincidence, but it's enough, more than enough, for me to surrender completely.

I feel Ali's fingers at my entrance. She slides them through the wetness that has gathered there. My body squirms with need, with pure want. But she's teasing me, looking at me there, making me wait. I'll have to pay her back for that.

"Ali, please," I beg, not caring how that makes me sound.

Then she finally slips her fingers inside of me. It feels like everything I've ever wanted—like the only thing I've wanted since I met her. But that can't be true. I can't let it be true. We're going to lead Lennox Breweries together. That's what I wanted, I remind myself.

There's nothing tentative about her strokes inside me. She means business. With her fingers inside me, she scoots up until her face hovers over mine. Once she's looking into my eyes, she starts fucking me again, and I'm about to lose it.

I try to keep my eyes open, to share this moment with her, to take in as much of her as I can as she fucks me, her fingers deep inside of me. All I can think, as I ride her fingers ever closer to orgasm, is that I'm hers. In that moment, she's got me, all of me. All of my attention is focused on her, all of my desire is wrapped around her fingers. Maybe this is what she wanted all along or maybe it just happened. Maybe I'll never know.

Something inside me gives, can no longer hold on, and a burning climax rips through me, throws my head against the pillow, has me screaming out her name. I come again and again, as though my body is making up for lost time, until my limbs sag against the bed and all I can do is utter a limp sigh.

"Oh, fuck," I mutter.

It takes a few moments before I can open my eyes again. I'm unsure of what I'm about to encounter. Will she give a smug grin? And if she does, will I be able to bear it?

But there's no smugness in Ali's expression when I look at her. There's only kindness and warmth and, perhaps, a little bit of doubt.

"That was amazing." I pull her to me, and as I do, something inside me already starts aching, because I know the night has only just begun, but whatever this is between us, is already ending.

25

ALI

When I wake, for a short moment, I think I'm in Singapore again. The room is unfamiliar and the other side of the bed is empty—I could be anywhere, really. But then I realize I'm at Jill's apartment. Before I get up and find her, I take a few seconds to savor the memory of last night. For all I know, once I clasp eyes on Jill, she'll tell me it was a huge mistake, and then that's all it will be for the rest of my life: a mere memory. At least now, I can still dream of more. Even I, someone who grew up with almost infinite possibilities, know that dreaming of more is futile. Perhaps in a moment of pending loss like this, I should be happy for the practice I've had.

Then another thought enters my head: did my father even make it through the night? Surely, if something had happened, someone would have called me. But it's an odd thought to have. I'm not used to thinking of my father first thing in the morning. Additionally, if he knew about this, he might feel like I disgraced the Lennox name even more than Sebastian has.

I hear water running somewhere. I'm still disoriented by this place. The running water sounds too far away to be in the bathroom. Jill must be in the kitchen. I look around for something to cover myself with. I find a navy-blue silk robe in the first closet I open. It feels worn and smells a bit musty, but it's only to cover up my body that smells of sex and exquisite orgasms had. I smile as I make my way into the kitchen, but make sure to rearrange my features when I greet Jill.

She looks at me as though I've just robbed her of something very valuable.

"Where did you find that?" she asks.

I assume she means the robe. "In the closet. I needed something to cover myself up with."

It's as if I can almost see the cogs in her brain whirring, like she's figuring out if, for some reason, it's okay for me to wear her old robe.

"It's not… mine," she says. "It used to belong to someone else."

"Sorry. I didn't know. And you were gone…" I have no idea how to behave. What I really want to do is go over and kiss her, but, perhaps for the first time ever in my life, I don't know if my kisses will be welcome—although they were more than welcome last night.

"I know we need to talk," Jill says curtly. "But I need to get to the office. I slept through my alarm."

"Alarm?" I didn't hear a thing this morning.

"Take a shower if you want. You probably need to go home before coming into work. I'll cover for you if Jeffrey wants to see you before you arrive."

"Can we just take one minute?" I do walk over to her now. "One breath?" I try a smile.

"Ali," she says on a sigh and shakes her head. "I don't know what to say. Clearly, this shouldn't have happened. If Jeffrey finds out, I'll be fired. You needed someone to comfort you last night, and I did, and it got out of hand. Do you think we can leave it at that?"

For someone who claims not to know what to say, she has a

lot of words at the ready. But what had I expected? That Jill was going to throw herself into a love affair with me? And is that even what I want?

She's staring at me, probably because I haven't answered her question. Do I want to leave it at this? *Can* I leave it at this? "For now." My voice croaks. I need a glass of water.

This is all a bit frosty for me, however. If I had my way, I would wrap my arms around her and at least claim one last hug. But this moment isn't about what I want—it's about respecting what Jill wants.

"Thank you." Her voice suddenly sounds much more heartfelt. Perhaps she had expected me to make a scene. I can hardly blame her for that expectation.

"I'll just shower at home." I can't stay here now. I understand where Jill is coming from, yet I feel the sharp sting of rejection.

I leave her in the kitchen and, unwashed, slip into the clothes I carelessly shed last night, like some sort of reverse playback of what occurred.

When I emerge from the bedroom again, Jill is standing firmly next to the kitchen counter.

"I'll see you at the office," I say, from the front door. As close as we were last night, this morning, the distance between us seems wholly unbridgeable. "Thanks for..." I don't want to sound too sheepish so I don't continue. And I can hardly thank her for her kindness when she gave me so much more.

I exit her apartment without even the possibility of touching Jill again. On the way to my house, the car already stuck in morning traffic, I call Evelyn and ask for my father's doctor's phone number. Because, at the moment, I have bigger fish to fry than to ascertain how I really feel about Jill. I need to convince my father he needs surgery—and he needs it this week. Before that, he needs to appoint Jill interim CEO.

Maybe sleeping with her now was very bad timing.

26

JILL

I FEEL LIKE AN IMPOSTER. Like someone with a secret that can never come out. It's as if I've betrayed the people I work with and, most of all, my boss, who also happens to be very sick—and whose sickness I feel like I have exploited in some way.

Jeffrey's not there yet and I remind myself that I'm not supposed to know about the gravity of his condition. How am I meant to focus on work when all my energy is going on concealing things? And not just that, but to processing that I slept with Ali.

I can't lie to myself and claim it wasn't utterly exhilarating—it was—but that doesn't make it okay. Of course it doesn't. And all the things I allowed myself not to feel last night, come rushing back to me now. Did I take advantage? Why did I even let her kiss me again? Is it all just a game to her?

"Are you all right?" Linda asks when she catches me daydreaming.

"It's going to be one of those days," I say.

"Is it?"

I wave off her question and close my office door. I have no idea how to get through the emotional minefield this day will be. A sensation keeps gnawing at me since this morning—since I sent Ali away. That I was too cold with Ali. Why couldn't my kindness, my compassion, extend to this morning? Because after last night, it wasn't only kindness anymore. It was way more than that.

Even though I have a million things to do, I'm waiting for things to happen. I'm waiting for Jeffrey to arrive; for Ali to arrive; to be told something, because I'm the COO of this company and I don't even officially know that my boss needs bypass surgery on his heart. I expected Jeffrey to have told me about something as significant as that, but he didn't, and maybe that fact sums up my relationship with him—and by extension, with this company. For someone who as good as turned his back on his family—out of grief, perhaps, but the reason isn't as important as the consequence—he suddenly seems very big on it. And I'm not, and never will be, family.

But I'm much closer to a member of the Lennox clan than he will ever realize. I shake off the thought, because it's inappropriate and also because it makes me think of Ali again. Of her scrumptious body. The look on her face when she came under my—*my!*—touch. Of how I felt this morning, before the panic set in, and I was basking in the afterglow of that glorious night we spent together. Those divine couple of minutes full of possibility.

Because I'm still waiting and my attention is too scattered to focus on anything right now, I indulge in fantasy. What's the worst that could happen? I envisage Ali and me going to her father's house together, as a couple. That's not a fantasy, I conclude. That's a flat-out nightmare. Add Sebastian to the picture with his relentless taunts and jibes, and the terror is complete. Our night together, glorious as it was, will have to remain a secret forever.

Then, finally, there's the familiar sounds in the hallway of the big boss arriving. The nervous tension ignites for a fraction. Everyone stands to greet him as though Jeffrey is a general who needs to be formally saluted every single morning.

Ali hasn't arrived yet.

I go into the hallway, keeping my face as expressionless as possible, because I'm not meant to know anything.

"My office in ten," Jeffrey says, his voice low, his complexion ashen.

I have ten minutes to pull it together. I go over things I usually talk to him about off the cuff, because they're my job and they're things I inherently know. I feel like I'm preparing for an exam, while all he probably wants is his daily briefing.

Then there's more noise in the corridor. Through the glass walls of my office I see Ali arrive. Her pace is brisk as she heads straight to her father's office, leaving me even more in the dark.

A few minutes later, Evelyn asks me to join them.

Showtime. I head into the boss's office.

I focus on Jeffrey, but it's actually quite hard to see him like this. Every single day, the lines on his face deepen and his eyes look more sunken, as though they're retreating—as though they've had enough. But I have to keep my focus on him because I can't even bear to look at Ali. Oh, how we have screwed this up royally. Sebastian walks in and closes the door behind him. For once, he succeeds in removing some tension from the room instead of recklessly adding to it.

"Okay," Jeffrey says. "Here's how it's going to be." He looks me in the eye. "My daughter has been talking to my doctor this morning." I'm not sure why Jeffrey's looking at me while he's talking about Ali. "They're ganging up on me, which leaves me no choice, Jill. I need you to step up for a while, just while I have surgery."

"Surgery?" I try to sound surprised.

"The old ticker's letting me down. It's nothing serious. I'll be back before you know it."

It's funny how he doesn't even ask if I want to be interim CEO. Everything's always automatically implied in Jeffrey Lennox's world.

"When are you having the surgery?" I ask.

"Friday. Bypass," he says curtly. "I'll be out for a week at least. Ideally, we wouldn't tell anyone, but in this day and age, it's too risky to keep a secret like that."

"A week?" Ali butts in. "A month more like, Dad." She shakes her head.

Jeffrey ignores her. "The point is, Jill, that I need you. I trust you to not fuck anything up while I'm gone."

"How are you feeling? Should you even be here today?"

"We need to distribute a press release," he says.

"Sure, but I'll take care of all of that. Jeffrey, you should go home and rest." I only dare to say these things because he looks like a man whose heart may actually give up on him any second now.

"I won't stay long," he says, much against my expectation. "We'll announce that you're taking over while I'm away. Meanwhile, keep prepping Ali, so we can have her approved by the board by the end of the month, as previously agreed."

"Can we, um…" I can barely get the words past the sudden lump in my throat. "Can someone else mentor Ali while I'm CEO?" I ask. I don't dare glance at Ali, but it's as though I can feel her shooting daggers into my back.

"Interim CEO," Sebastian says. "I'll do it."

"Hell, no," Ali says. "I should follow Jill, especially now that she's going to be *interim* CEO."

"Everything stays as it was," Jeffrey says. "Now go and do some work."

"Nice try," Ali whispers in my ear as I exit Jeffrey's office.

27

ALI

I BARGE into Jill's office without asking permission. I convinced my father to make her interim CEO so he could have his surgery and she just tried to get rid of me in the process, her cowardly attempt to do so tacked on like an after-thought. And after the night we spent together.

"That wasn't very nice," I say.

"Please close the door." Jill sits behind her desk. She looks a little tired. I did keep her up all night. She waits until the door is firmly closed to speak again. "How am I supposed to work with you now?" She puffs out some air. "Fuck, Ali. What have we done?"

"We slept together," I state the obvious.

"I didn't expect it to be so hard in front of them." She nods at the wall that separates her office from my father's.

"I'm sure you'll be able to handle yourself again in no time." I sound the exact opposite of how I feel. I'm touched that Jill could barely hold it together. But I need to remember her words from this morning. And how she just tried to get rid of me.

"I just wanted… a little break from you. I need it, Ali. I've just been put in charge. Your father's undergoing surgery this week. There are so many people I need to speak with."

"I'm not going anywhere, Jill." And it's just as hard for me. "So use me. Tell me what to do to help. Throw me in at the deep end." Maybe work will consume me so much, I'll forget about last night entirely. If only it hadn't been so spectacular. If only I wasn't already consumed with the desire to do it again.

"Don't tell anyone about this, please? That includes your friend Madison. If this comes out, it can and will be used against us and then we can kiss our leadership of this company goodbye."

I do understand that the stakes are higher for Jill, that this is harder for her to even entertain as a possibility. But still. "I won't tell anyone," I lie. I already know I'll tell Madison. I might go nuts if I don't. Madison will surely go through the roof when I tell her.

"I suppose I shouldn't invite you to my house tonight then?" I say.

Jill shakes her head. "The sooner we can pretend this never happened, the better." As she sits there saying these words—rejecting me—inside me, the desire for her just grows.

"Jill, please. We are flesh and blood with feelings. At least I am."

"Did I…" She can't even look me in the eye anymore. "Tell me honestly, Ali, did I take advantage of the situation? Because if I did, it surely wasn't my intention."

"Of course you didn't. I kissed *you,* remember?"

"But I'm the one who should have known better."

"Stop it, Jill. All this talk of moving on and forgetting about it. Is that really what you want?"

"It's not about what I want. There's no choice here, Ali. I hope you realize that."

"There's always a choice."

"Maybe there is in your world, but I've worked for this

moment for a long time. I may only be CEO for a brief time, but for me, it's a really big deal, regardless of the circumstances. This is our moment. This is when we start making our strategic moves so this company will be ours."

"Wow." It's back to business for Jill already. Although I know that she wasn't the one to take advantage of the situation, this is all working out rather well for her.

"I don't mean to be insensitive," she says. "I care about Jeffrey and, in the end, I want some sort of happy ending for Sebastian as well, but you and I, we're the future of—"

"Jill, please," I interrupt her. "Stop. Just stop. Look at me." I force her to hold my gaze. "Everything is different now. I'm not some heartless bitch driven only by ambition. Have you even for a minute stopped to consider that I might genuinely care for you?"

She scoffs. "There's no room for feelings here."

"For fuck's sake! Who is this sitting in front of me today? She has nothing to do with the woman I was with last night."

"I know I'm twenty-four hours too late with this, and what's done is done, but you have to stop this now, Ali. I mean it. As soon as your father leaves, go be with him. That's what should be important for you right now."

"Did you forget he just ordered you to mentor me further?"

"And I will, just not today. I need you out of my sight today. I need to process and I need to work."

The sting behind my eyes surprises me. I had no idea Jill could be so cold, although she already gave me a taste of that this morning.

"Are you for real?" I tap the tip of my shoe against the floor.

"Ali, please." Her voice sounds pleading—even more so than when she begged me to fuck her last night. "This is hard for me as well."

"Okay." I have no choice but to respect her wishes. And she's right. I should spend the rest of the day with my father, or at least try to. I can give her the day, because there's always tomorrow, and the day after, and the one after.

I leave Jill and, before returning to my father's office, where I'm not sure I'll even be welcome, I stop by Sebastian's.

"Are you okay?" I ask, thinking that my life was so much easier before I returned to L.A., regardless of the reason why I left. Now I have Jill to deal with. And my dad's health. And my brother's jealousy.

"Fine. Just worried about Dad."

"And about Jill?"

He fixes his gaze on me at the mention of Jill's name. "It makes sense for now," he says, then shrouds himself in silence.

I can't help but wonder what Leah would have made of all of this. Jill had been in my father's employ for ten years by the time Leah died, but I can't remember us ever discussing her. Leah and I were far too busy hating the family business and vowing we'd never have anything to do with it, because in our view, it took away the only parent we still had.

I can only think of Leah as a twenty-five-year old woman, who would have very different views on life than I have now, so her imagined opinion isn't of great importance. Still, I'd like to think that at least my sister would have understood. And if she were still alive, at least I would have been able to tell her. So many of my secrets died with Leah. Things I only ever told her. I still keep her secrets and I intend to take them to my grave with me as well.

28

JILL

THIS IS IT. This is the moment I've been waiting for. The word 'interim' is easy enough to drop or forget or simply pretend is not there. I'm CEO of Lennox Breweries. The press release has been sent out. The phones are ringing off the hook, but I'm not taking any of those calls today. Jeffrey has gone home. Ali somehow convinced him to put his health first, but, in the end, he didn't have much choice. If not, there wouldn't be anything left to put first.

I should be over the moon. I should be making plans to celebrate—discreetly of course, keeping Jeffrey's health in mind. Surely he'll need me to step in for a few months, rather than weeks. This stint as CEO, added to my 6 years of experience as COO, and my additional 15 years at this company, will make my market value balloon. I will get offers once Ali takes over—if she does. My future can be considered secure. Apart from that, I've never spent much of the money I've made. It's all squirreled away in investments. I'm already rich. Even if the worst happened, and I got fired, I'd easily survive. I would only have to live with the dents in my ego and reputation.

But this whole thing with Ali gnaws at me and, instead of

taking Linda and my team out for drinks, I just go home. On the evening after the day when I've been appointed CEO, I have nothing better to do than to sit in Los Angeles traffic, inhale the smog, honk at other drivers, and wonder what the hell I'm doing.

Because if I can't celebrate this special occasion with anyone special, if I shoulder life's burdens *and* joys all on my own, then what's the fucking point? I can call my parents and I'm sure they'll be proud, but they were already proud of me. I can watch CNBC tonight and see what's being said about me, but that's not my style.

Instead, I have to try to keep my mind off Ali, which is doubly hard, because, if last night hadn't happened, she would be the one I'd be celebrating with. She's the one I have further plans with. She's the one who made it happen. She forced her father's hand—in everyone's best interest. An act befitting of a future CEO.

But I can't call Ali. Instead, I was so distant with her, so harsh, first this morning in my apartment—which I'm beginning to dread returning to—and then in my office. And it was so hard. So the exact opposite of what I really wanted to do. But I had no choice. Of course someone like Ali believes there are always choices, but in this case, there really aren't. The only other possible option is a secret affair, but that's simply too risky. And then how will it end? A secret affair is not a future. It's just a temporary giving-in to indulgence, and I think I've already done enough of that.

Traffic is completely blocked because of an accident—making me think of Leah, making me think of Ali—and I'm beginning to wonder if I'll ever make it to my place tonight. Maybe sitting home alone isn't what I need after all. I briefly consider Dolly's, but I can't face that. And what would another woman's touch do, even if I get lucky? Erase Ali's? As if that's even possible.

Instead, I maneuver myself toward the exit ramp, earning myself numerous frustrated honks from other drivers and two screamed mentions of the word 'bitch'. When I'm off the freeway, I pull over and google the address of Matriciana's. It's ultra-private there and the cocktails are divine.

When I hand the valet my car keys, I'm reminded that I let Ali drive away in her own car that night. She must have been over the limit. But is everything my responsibility now? After what happened to her sister, you'd think she'd be much more careful. I make my way to the basement and am faced with a closed door. The password. Damn. I consider leaving but why should only the likes of Ali be allowed inside this place? I knock and the door swings open.

"Password," a very broad-shouldered guy says. Where's man-bun when you need him?

"I don't know the password, but I was here not long ago with Ali Lennox." For crying out loud. If Ali knew I was using her name to get into this place, she'd surely use it against me until the end of our days.

"Is she here?"

"No, it's just me."

"Ali's not coming?" the guy says, as if he knows her personally. Maybe he does.

"She's not," I confirm.

"I can't let you in just because you know Ali Lennox. For all I know, you could be lying." He squints at me.

"I swear to you, I was here with her…" I try to remember. "Two weeks ago? Three? Ask the server with his hair—"

"FaceTime her and I'll let you in," he says.

"What?"

"Call her and make sure I can see her."

I roll my eyes. Why can't he just let me in? It's not as if there's a long queue of people whose space I'd be taking up.

"Is that really necessary?"

"I'm afraid it is." He looks at me triumphantly, as though he has me all sussed out—and someone like me wouldn't know the likes of Ali Lennox at all. I consider asking if calling Sebastian Lennox would work, but I don't want to argue with this guy anymore.

"I'm the new CEO of Lennox Breweries," I try. It sounds so lame under the circumstances.

"Good for you." He folds his arms in front of his chest, as if to say: you're never getting past me, old lady.

Today of all days, I can't let this hipster gorilla get the best of me. Getting inside this cocktail bar is about to become a point of personal pride. How dare he suggest I don't know Ali Lennox—this time last night, I was in bed with her.

Through my building rage, I manage to call Ali. She picks up after two rings.

"Jill?" she asks.

"Hey, um..." Oh, Jesus. "Ali, sorry to disturb you. Can you switch on your camera real quick, please? Some guy who gets a kick out of denying middle-aged ladies entry to a bar needs confirmation that I know you."

"What?" I can hear the smile in Ali's voice.

"I'm at that cocktail bar we went to together, but they won't let me in," I whisper.

"Leave it with me. Give him your phone. I'll abracadabra you inside in no time."

Ali appears on my screen and I show it to the Neanderthal guarding the door as though this club is his most precious property and people like me should never be allowed in.

"This is Ali Lennox," I hear her say. "Jill Gold is my boss and my friend. If you would be so kind to grant her entrance to your establishment, please."

"Of course, Miss Lennox." He opens the door wide and, suddenly, he's all smiles; all the menace has left his demeanor.

I'm so incensed, I just want to leave, but I can't give him that satisfaction now.

"Thanks," I say to Ali.

"Switch on your camera," Ali says. "You owe me that."

"For this? Come on. I just needed your name, Ali."

"That might be so, but without it, you wouldn't be sipping from the most delicious cocktail in town."

With a sigh, I touch the camera icon.

"It's only fair I can see you too." She smiles at me. "What are you doing there?"

"I needed a drink. And that guy was being such an asshole."

"It's his job," Ali says matter-of-factly. "Anyway, glad to be of service. Have one on me."

"How's your father?"

"Grumpy," she says. "Being on the cusp of heart surgery is making him even more cranky than usual."

"Tell him I'll stop by the house tomorrow."

"You'll do no such thing, Jill. He needs to rest."

"Okay." This is not the time or place to argue with Ali. And she's probably right. "Good night then."

"Have fun, Jill. Don't drink too much. No hangover in the office tomorrow." She sends me one last pixelated smile, then hangs up.

29

ALI

THIRTY MINUTES after Jill's call, I'm standing in front of the guy I spoke to via FaceTime. He opens the door without me having to say anything.

"Is Jill Gold still here?" I ask.

He just nods and ushers me in. I'm a little nervous when I approach Jill's booth, but how else could I interpret her call other than as an invitation? A convoluted one, but still very much an open invitation. Why else would she call me out of the blue like that?

"Hey." I paint on my warmest smile.

"Ali?" The surprise in her glance makes me question my interpretation skills. "What are you doing here?"

I feel a bit on display, so I slide into the booth.

"You called me."

"Well, yes, to get into this wretched place."

I tilt my head. "This isn't the only cocktail bar in L.A., you know."

"I know." She sighs. "It's silly. That guy just really pushed the wrong button on the wrong day. I had forgotten about the stupid password and..." She rolls her eyes. "I'm sorry for the confusion. I can see how that might have happened. I didn't mean to—"

"It's fine." I need to get over my disappointment quickly. "Now that I'm here, do you mind if I have a drink with you? Or would you prefer me to sit in another booth?" It sounds a little facetious, but still—she called me.

"Don't be silly." She pushes her empty cocktail glass away from her. "Of course, we can have a drink together."

"How many of those have you had?"

She shrugs. "Enough to feel a whole lot better." Her smile is a bit leery. "Enough to be genuinely happy that you're here."

I gesture for the server to stop by. It's the same guy as last time. I order the same as Jill's having, plus a large bottle of water and some snacks. She looks like she needs some food in her, pronto.

"Were you upset?" I ask once the server has gone. It's a bit of a trip to sit here again with her. So much seems to have happened since we were last here. I feel very differently about Jill now that she has shown me the other side of her—the sexy, hot, screaming-when-she-comes side. I'll never see her again the way I saw her that night we were first at this bar.

She pulls her lips into that typical Jill pout. "I was feeling sorry for myself. I don't even know why I came here."

"You became CEO today, Jill. You should be celebrating."

She shrugs again. "That would feel like dancing on Jeffrey's grave very prematurely. It's all so… ambivalent. Of course, I'm happy that he trusted me to lead the company during his illness. But, well, you know."

"Tell me."

"Tell you what?" Her eyes are watery when she stares at me.

"Tell me what it is I'm supposed to know."

"But you already know."

"Jill." I lean over the table and bring my face as close to hers as I can. She doesn't flinch, but that could just be the alcohol slowing her down. "Talk to me." I've seen you naked, I think. But you can see a person naked a dozen times and still not have really seen them.

"I did want to have a celebratory drink," she says, sounding very clear suddenly. "With you. Only I couldn't. Maybe that's why I ended up here of all places. Because you brought me here and maybe I stupidly believed I could summon your spirit." She scoffs, then regroups. "Ali, what we did last night... that doesn't happen to me very often. Even though I know it was wrong and it was all just a consequence of the circumstances, but..." She falls silent again.

"But what?" I nudge her.

"But all I can think about..." She cuts her gaze to me again, her blue eyes a little dim, a little glazed over. "Is doing it again."

My heart surges. My pulse picks up speed.

"Then why don't you?"

"Because... you *know* why. I'm not going to repeat myself over and over again."

The server comes over and presents us with our order. Jill goes straight for a cheese stick.

"I don't have the answers here, but let me tell you this." I hold up my cocktail. "I feel exactly the same way."

She bursts into a chuckle, but she holds her glass aloft as well. "How can you?"

"Why would you even question that? We were both there last night. We both know exactly what it was like."

"That may be so, but... whatever I represent to you at this time in your life, I realize it's like that for a reason. I roped you into my plan on your first day back at head office. And we had... some moments, that we each interpreted in our own way. I won't pretend to know you, Ali, but I can understand why you'd fool yourself into believing you want to be with me."

"Fool myself?" It's my turn to utter an incredulous chuckle. "Who do you take me for?"

"I take you for what I see that you are. Someone who came home to what's left of her family—a family she's not particularly close to—only to find her father in poor health, and her brother struggling too. You must also be flooded with the memories of your sister. It would make anyone a little… fragile."

"Jesus Christ, Jill." Alcohol seems to do funny things to her. She's more open with me than she's been before, but it's not an analysis of myself I'm after. Especially not the cobbled-together, drunken one she has just given me. "Let me put it as plainly as I can." I take a breath. "I like you. It's as simple as that. I've liked you from day one. I kissed you twice, remember?"

"How am I supposed to take that seriously?"

"You took it very seriously last night."

"That's different. That was sex."

"So? Are you trying to say that some of it was fake?"

"No… you're not getting it. It's not just that you're Jeffrey's daughter and Sebastian's sister. You're almost twenty years younger than me. You could have anyone you wanted."

I hold up my hand to stop her. "Clearly not, because I want you."

Finally, something akin to a smile appears on her face. "But why? Why *me*?"

"Because, Jill Gold," I take a sip from my cocktail, "you've worked with my family for such a long time, yet you have this kindness in you. It took me by surprise that you would be so warm and thoughtful with me. The conversations we've had about Leah, however brief, I've never had with my father or with Sebastian. Granted, I did skip town, but I did so for a reason. Several reasons, in fact. To not constantly be reminded of Leah in this city where we spent so much time together, but also to get away from Dad and Sebastian. My brother may accuse me of running away, and that's fine, because I did run away, and maybe that was cowardly, but I also did it because I didn't feel like I had a choice." I didn't mean to go there again, but Jill seems to have that effect on me. More than anyone, by just being her, she's helped me to move forward so much. If only I could put that into words for her—and show her how much that means to me. But it seems as though I don't have the language for it yet. So I'm only left with the pulsing desire to lean in and kiss her again.

"I appreciate that, Ali," she says. "But I don't really know what to do with that."

"Do I wish I'd met you under different circumstances?" I say. "Maybe, but—"

"But that's just it," Jill interrupts me. "Under different circumstances, you would never have looked at me twice."

"You don't know that. And life is made up of our circumstances. This is what we have. This is who life has made us." I pull up my shoulders. "I will never be a woman who grew up with a mother. I will never be someone who grows old with her twin sister by her side. They're gone. That's done. And their deaths have become part of who I am." I draw a deep breath to stop my voice shaking.

"Maybe, one day, I'll get along better with Sebastian." Now that the words have started, they won't stop. "Maybe he'll shed his cloak of douchebaggery someday. Or maybe I'll find it in my heart to see him for who he truly is: just a boy who lost his mother, who can't even remember her because he was only three years old when she died. He lost a sister as well. And he had to manage without a father because for Dad the brewery became everything. And even that I can understand, you know? In my better moments, I can understand them both, and I can only hope that they do the same of me."

I shake my head. "Fuck, Jill. Can't you see? This is what you do to me. I don't talk this way to anyone else. To no one. Not even to Madison, because I left her as well. She built her own life while I was away, without me, and starting over with someone is always different than starting fresh."

"You do love a speech, Ali," Jill says.

"Only with you. Something about you makes the words tumble right out of me." I pour us both some much-needed water—for me, because my mouth is dry and for Jill, because as much as I like it when she's tipsy and less uptight, at the end of this, I will want her closer to sober. "Now let me ask *you* a question. The same question, in fact… Why me?"

"W—why you?" Jill sips greedily from the water. "You kissed me. Twice."

"I can't accept that as an answer. Surely you don't get involved with anyone who tries to kiss you?"

"I'm not sure I have an answer. I just have… all these feelings. I just… I want you so much. I didn't allow myself to think about that. Not until you kissed me again last night. I can't tell you why because I didn't let myself think about that either. Doing that would be legitimizing what we did and I don't think that's a very good idea."

"Of course it is." I grow bolder again. "I think you should legitimize it as soon as possible, because, Jill, how on earth are we going to stop it happening again?" The smile on my lips is wide and audacious.

"That's why," Jill says. "That right there, what you just did, that's why I want you so much. You're so… I don't know how to say it. You have this enormous lust for life and you just grab what you want. At first, it annoyed the hell out of me, but now I can't help but admire it. After all that has happened to you, you've still managed to become this joyous, radiant person. I'm very drawn to that."

My lips form into a smile. There's only one thing I can think of right now. I want her again. I need her. The question is, how am I going to get her out of this bar? I don't want to take advantage of her when she's clearly tipsy. Then again, she's certainly lucid enough to have a very revealing conversation with. And what she just said hasn't only made my heart swell.

"Thank you for sharing that," I say, while my mind races trying to come up with a plan.

She looks me in the eye, the blue of her glance a little clearer than before, her lips pursed, accentuating the fullness of them. "Do you want to get out of here?"

30

JILL

WE'VE both left our cars and in the taxi I make a note in my phone to remind myself in the morning where my car is. I also need something to do with my hands, hoping the movement will keep my mind from spinning out of control too much. Because what the hell am I doing? Why am I in a taxi with Ali? Actually, we are only in the taxi. I could ask to be dropped at my place and send Ali on her way. But it's the very last thing I want to do. I want her near. I don't want to sleep with her again, I tell myself. Surely, I'm old and wise enough to resist that temptation.

I glance at her from the corner of my eye, as though afraid that if I turn my face toward her fully, all will already be lost. And of course I'm fooling myself. Of course I asked her back to my place because all I want to do is sleep with her again, because I want her to make me feel the way she did last night again.

"Are you all right?" she asks.

I do turn toward her now and I catch sight of her hand sneaking toward me. It's on the seat, just next to my thigh, like an invitation. All I have to do is grab it to make my intentions known, to let her know we're on the same page. And of course we want the same thing. I haven't felt this close to another person since… I can't even remember. And the fact that I don't remember says it all. So I tell myself, while my hand travels toward hers, that I can allow myself one more night with Ali Lennox. A two-night stand. Because, sometimes, once isn't enough. I need another night with her to get her out of my system. After that, even though I might want her even more, I'll need to be much stronger than this. It's all that bouncer's fault. If only he had let me in without all his posturing. Tomorrow, I won't be going to any hidden, hipster cocktail bars to which I can only be granted access through Ali. Tomorrow, Thursday, Ali will be with her father—if he allows it. She'll be nervous about his surgery. She's probably already nervous right now, what with how easily death seems to visit her family.

"You did a hell of a thing." I take her hand in mine. "Convincing your father to have the surgery."

"He needed the right person to tell him. Someone who's not just on his payroll. Someone who's not trying to grovel their way back into his good graces like Sebastian."

"Still. It can't have been easy."

Ali shrugs. "I didn't want him sacrificing his health for this company even more than he already has. I know it's his life's work and LB was his saving grace after Mom died, but, come on…"

"Maybe that's one of the reasons he asked you to come back. Because he knew that only you would be able to tell him what to do when the time came."

"Jill." She squeezes my hand. "Can we not talk about my father for a bit?"

"Of course." I squeeze back and look out of the window. Traffic's still pretty jammed up, but at least we're moving, albeit at a slow pace. My building's not too far from here.

"Can I ask you something… that you may not want to answer?"

"That sounds ominous." I look back at her and in the passing light that illuminates her face, then obscures it for a second again, I see that she's tired too. That coming back and facing her family—and dealing with her father—has left a mark. "But yes, ask away." I don't feel as though I can refuse her anything, not tonight.

"What happened with you and the woman in the picture? Melissa, was it?"

"Wow." I grin at her. "You're so much cleverer than I would ever have given you credit for. You ask me this question when I have nowhere to go and I've had a bit too much to drink and you've just shared another piece of yourself with me."

"You make it sound so premeditated, Jill, while it's not. It's called a conversation, I believe. I share things. You share things. That's how these things work."

"Fair enough." I look out of the window again, as though the streetlights that glide by can help me find the words. "I thought Melissa was the love of my life. I still think of her like that sometimes because I haven't met anyone who's been able to convince me otherwise, but if she really is—was—the love of my life, then I guess I'm not really cut out for much of a love life."

"What happened?"

"She loved me and then she didn't." Even though it's been decades, a cold fist still closes around my heart when I think about it. "In a lot of ways, I reacted to the loss the way your father did after he lost your mother. I moved west and worked and worked and worked, to not have to deal with my emotions. I think Jeffrey recognized that in me." I realize I'm talking about Jeffrey again, while the subject should be Melissa. But Ali doesn't say anything. She just lets me speak. "When someone you love with every fiber of your being stops loving you, when that becomes clear to you, it's... uh, well, it hurts. When she told me that... she'd basically fallen out of love with me, it hurt like nothing had hurt me before. And I'm sure it says something about me, about my personality, that I wasn't able to deal with it very well. And that I haven't really allowed myself to fall for anyone else since. It has been a hell of a long time." I take a deep breath. "But, you know, it is what it is. Over the years, I've adjusted to being single very well. It just works for me. It makes sense with the life I lead, with what I've committed to at LB."

"I'm sorry that happened to you," Ali says.

"It happens to everyone, doesn't it? It's a rite of passage. You need to have your heart broken and your soul crushed, I guess, to develop life skills—and thick skin." I'd never imagined myself in the back of a taxi, slowly cruising through the big boulevards of Los Angeles, holding hands with a much younger woman, talking about Melissa. But it feels good to finally say it out loud to someone. And to know, once and for all, that I survived the heartache, even though, at times, I felt as though the smallest, most insignificant things would remind me of her forever.

"She must be some woman, that Melissa," Ali says, "that she managed to break your heart like that."

"She was. Is. She's married with children now. Lives in Westchester. The suburban dream and all that."

"Oh Christ, what a nightmare." Ali smiles, and I don't know if she says it because it's how she really feels or to make me feel better.

"I used to believe we all wanted the same things, but we don't. I never wanted children. Maybe I would have if Melissa and I had stayed together. I don't know." I think about what Ali said earlier about how our circumstances make us into who we are. "Maybe I would have been happy in suburbia. Who knows?"

"You wouldn't have met me." Ali's smile has turned into a grin.

"There's that." I reciprocate her grin. "And I wouldn't be so shockingly rich."

"Jill Gold." She pulls my hand toward her. "Are you saying that being rich is more fulfilling than having children?"

"That's really not for me to say, since I've never had children. I haven't always been rich, though, and I quite like it." My hand is in Ali's lap. "Do you want children?"

"I'm not sure. Most days, I still feel like I'm twenty-five. Like I stopped getting older the day Leah died. And I think I have all the time in the world to decide, but then it hits me that I'm actually ten years older. Although, granted, I often live like a twenty-five-year-old."

Her thumb caresses my palm and I feel it everywhere. I've stopped paying attention to the traffic and I'm surprised when the taxi stops outside my building.

In the elevator to the top floor, Ali's hand still clasped in mine, I conclude that it was good to talk to Ali—different than anyone else I talk to—but I don't think much more talking will be accomplished tonight.

31

ALI

I'M BRIEFLY DRAWN to the vista out of Jill's penthouse window, but then I only have eyes for her. She behaves a little bit differently when she's in her home. She's a touch more relaxed, not so measured. Of course, that could also be the alcohol. And the fact that we've already slept together. Then I'm hit with the memory of this morning, when she kicked me out of here, and it feels like a memory I need to undo straight away.

"Are you going to boot me out again in the morning?" I prop my butt against the windowsill.

She walks toward me. "I didn't know you were staying."

Because I'm half-sitting, our faces are at the same height for once and I take the opportunity to stare deep into her eyes. "I think you'll find me very hard to get rid of." I pull her toward me. "I won't be dismissed that easily again, Jill."

"Do we have to talk about tomorrow morning already?" She shuffles forward, forcing my legs to spread. "Because I don't want today to be over yet." She narrows her eyes a fraction, then tilts her head, and kisses me. First, I feel relief that she's the one initiating the kiss for once, but then, when her kiss deepens and she presses herself closer to me, all I feel is how much I want her again. The memories of last night flood my brain. Of her initial reticence, which was quickly replaced by the most addictive abandon. I want to see her like that again. I want to feel her body yield under my touch again.

She retreats for a fraction of a second, looks me in the eye, then leans back in and kisses me on the neck. She kisses a path to my ear, and whispers, "I want you so fucking much." And with that, her hand travels from my arm to my breast. She squeezes it—my nipple stands to attention immediately. She breathes heavily into my ear. "I think I'll have you here."

I burst into a chuckle. She can have me wherever she wants. Maybe we can do this at the office some time. But no, I'm pushing things too far again, and Jill's hand is traveling down and a finger hooks itself under the button of my pants.

I love how uninhibited she is off the bat—it must be the loosening effect of the booze—whereas last time, she had some serious qualms to deal with. Or just maybe, this is how she is the second time around. We've had our first time. Now, we continue. I'm curious what tonight will be like and as Jill's finger slips deeper into my pants, I get the inkling that she very much wants to be in charge.

I let her because why would I even want to argue with her about that? Jill admitted that she has denied herself so much over the years, so I'll let her have anything that she wants of me.

And I want what she wants. I want her finger much deeper in my pants, clawing at my underwear. I'm ready for whatever she has to bring, for whatever she wants to give me, because one thing I've learned about Jill is that when she's in a giving mood—which might not last very long, only the length of a very short night—she gives it all.

Then her hand retreats from my pants and she starts undoing my blouse buttons. She starts with the bottom one and works her way to the top, slowly revealing my skin to the night sky and the glittering lights outside, but also to her own gaze, which lights up more with each button she undoes.

"You're so fucking gorgeous," she mumbles. I don't think she's saying it to me—I can barely make out the words. She's talking to herself, which is, in many ways, much more arousing.

She makes quick work of my bra and gazes at my breasts as if they're the eighth wonder of the world. Exposed to the air, my nipples are hard, like they're reaching out for her touch. She stares at me as though she needs to have a long hard think about what she's going to do to me, and I'm reminded of her question: why me?

As if that's even a question that can ever be adequately answered. But it's not just her kindness that has me craving Jill's touch. Right now, her kindness has nothing do with it. It's the way her face changes when she looks at me. It's how she sees me, and how her view of me has changed. I've had to change my own view of myself over the years. It's taken me a very long time to find the person I once was underneath the rubble of my grief. It has taken thousands of nights of escape, of loud thumping music that obscured the longing in my own heartbeat, of waking up in other countries, in other beds, in other places Leah and I would never get to share. But all the while, I felt like she was there with me and it was my duty to take her along, even though she was dead and she'd never go anywhere again. I felt like I had to live a life so stuffed with events and people and parties that it would be good enough for the two of us. A life I tried to continue when I came back to Los Angeles but that Jill, without knowing it, has pressed the pause button on.

Jill finally comes for my breasts. She cups them in her hands, and pinches my nipples between her fingers. When she looks up at me, only able for a split second, it seems, to tear away her attention from my chest, I see her yearning so clearly, and it's so different than the desire I've seen in the eyes of all the women I've slept with over the years. Not because the intention behind it is different, but the sentiment and the person are. Here's a woman who wraps herself in turtleneck sweaters because she believes it might save her from her own desires, from her own sexual aliveness—she's wearing one right now, because of course she needed to hide herself after what we did last night.

And look at her now. She's still wearing all her clothes but she couldn't be more naked, she couldn't be more revealed to me as she is in this moment. Even though I'm half-seated, my knees buckle a little when she sucks a nipple between her lips, when she bites it playfully and smiles up at me after, and I see that aliveness brimming in her gaze. I know then that she won't be able to do again what she did this morning. We've crossed over into another realm—the one where we're actually doing this. Jill may not know this yet, but I seem to have a knack for figuring things out before she does.

While she feasts on my nipples, both her hands slide down my belly, toward my pants again. Without further ado, she unzips me. She lets go of my nipple and tugs all the clothes I'm still wearing down, exposing me completely. I kick off my shoes and step out of my pants and panties until I stand naked before her, my back to the L.A. night.

She hoists her sweater over her head and then drops to her knees. She inhales deeply, as though steadying herself, then glances up at me. The smile she sends me is warm but also quick with impatience and lust. At the sight of her, kneeling before me like this, I swallow hard, as though my growing desire has gathered as a lump in my throat.

I bring my hands to her hair as she slants forward and without so much as a stray kiss on my thigh as a lead-up, as foreplay, she locks her lips on my clit. The touch shoots all the way up my spine, awakening an extra layer of lust at the base of my skull. It ripples in a hot wave of want and abandon as I press her closer to me, as I spread my legs wider, as I push myself toward her to meet more of her delicious tongue.

My body gives into Jill immediately, as if it's already so familiar with her it instinctively knows what to do—let go and enjoy. She licks my clit and, instantly, all my nerve endings light up. I turn my head to the side, and through half-closed lids, with my cheek pressed against the window, I catch a glimpse of the city below. It pulses and blinks and it reflects the fireworks going on inside me, at the touch of Jill's tongue against me, at the eagerness with which she came for me, as though she never had any other choice in life but to do just that.

Then I feel her fingertip skate up my inner thigh, as a prelude, no doubt, and something inside me already convulses, crunches around nothing in sheer anticipation. She frees my clit from the electrifying touch of her tongue, while her finger slips and slides through the wetness between my legs. Then she's fucking me. She gives me a few slow, tentative strokes, but then, there's only intention left, when she drives her fingers high and quick inside of me. I have to look down, have to see the look in her eyes.

Her mouth's slightly agape with effort and, perhaps, wonder at how we're doing this again so quickly. But sometimes, I tell myself, two people have no choice. She may claim she only needed me to get into that cocktail bar, but I call bullshit—although I won't be telling her that any time soon.

Jill's eyes are wide when she looks up at me and I could be making it up but it's as though I can see the pleasure in her glance, the kick she gets out of fucking me—the one person she shouldn't be fucking. Her pleasure mirrors mine, augments it, multiplies it, but not more so than when her glance cuts away and I watch as she fixes her gaze, and her intentions, on my clit.

The next thing I know, she's licking me again and her

fingers push inside me. I have to remove my hands from her hair so I can hold on to the windowsill for fear of crashing to the floor.

When I come, I call her name until it reverberates inside me. It's so short, so compact, like her.

I'm not much closer to knowing what this is, what she has loosened inside me, but in that moment, as the last of my orgasm crashes through me, it's tempting to think this is the closest to love I've come in a long, long time.

32

JILL

WHEN I WAKE UP, a surge of panic hits me again, but I don't run from the bed the way I did yesterday. I take a few deep breaths and let the memories of last night warm me and make me feel alive, instead of letting them push me into frantic business mode—and treat Ali like she's just a silly mistake I made.

Because she's not. She's the woman I've shared my bed with two nights in a row. While her shape is unfamiliar in my bed, waking up next to her, when I really let myself revel in it, is such a joy. It makes me a little heady. Giddy even. Then I throw an arm around her because it's what I should have done yesterday. I press myself against her, inhale her morning musky sex scent, to make up for what I lacked yesterday.

And still she said that it was my warmth that drew her to me. It's a warmth I only seem to have for her, and only under certain circumstances. A warmth I want to inundate her with, as she's still sleeping, and lies here looking almost innocent—although I know she's far from innocent.

"Hey." She turns on her back and blinks open her eyes. "You're still here," she says.

"I am."

"What time is it?"

"It doesn't matter. I'm the boss now."

She chuckles. "What do you have in mind for me today, boss?"

"This." I lean in and kiss her and it's a sober, morning kiss, making it very different from all the other kissing we have done so far, under the light of muted lamps and the influence of expensive cocktails. And still, it makes me feel exactly the same as an evening kiss—like I never want to stop kissing her. So much for getting this—her—out of my system. Sleeping with her again has had the opposite effect.

She shakes her head when we break from the kiss.

"What?"

"I should have known to pack some spare clothes when you called me last night," she says.

"How could you have?"

"Because, Jill, you're actually quite predictable." She grins widely.

"Maybe I am, but you couldn't have foreseen what happened. I certainly didn't."

She shrugs and sits up, the sheet tumbling off her. Her breasts are exposed and I have to restrain myself from reaching for them—but instant and permanent access to her magnificent breasts is a privilege I've not yet earned for myself.

"I'm not kicking you out," I say softly, "but that only means I'm being more of an adult about this. Not much else has changed."

She turns to me. "I'll tell you what has changed. My father's being admitted to hospital today to have heart surgery tomorrow. Let's face it, with the luck we have in our family, he might never wake up again. He might die, Jill. And then why would we have even hesitated to be together?"

I throw an arm around her. "Hey, Jeffrey's going to be just fine."

"I don't remember much from that time, but I do remember that's what my dad used to say before Mom died. And she still died."

I pull her a little closer. "The surgery he's having is performed a million times every day around the world. It's routine. He'll be up and grumping again in no time." What else can I say? I don't share Ali's realism and isn't it my main task, this morning in this bed, to support her?

She shrugs again, and I take it as my cue to remove my arm from around her shoulders.

"I wonder if he's scared right now," she says.

"He would never show it, but I'm sure he is," I say.

Ali pulls the sheet around her body. "After Mom died, he just pulled away from us. He replaced our presence in his life with the brewery, as if he didn't need us anymore. It's probably more complicated than that. For all I know, he was protecting himself, immunizing himself against another loss. And then he —we—lost Leah and I sort of knew I'd lost him as well. Not that I had much of him before. I mean, I always had his money. And I knew I would always have a job at the brewery, although, for the longest time I didn't want to work for LB, because I felt it took from me. But now, I might actually lose him. He might die." She brings the edge of the sheet to the corner of her eye.

"Go be with him today. It's the only thing you can do."

She nods. "I'll call Sebastian. We should both be with him, although he won't want us there."

"He may say he doesn't, but he does. He has no choice, either way." I find her hand under the sheet and take it in mine. "If he protests, tell him the interim CEO has ordered it."

She looks at me, her eyes all watery and pink. "Thanks for being here. For making it easier."

"You don't have to do everything on your own." Tears prick behind my eyes as well.

"That's what it has felt like since Leah died. I sometimes

resented her for always being with me, but she was there, you know. Even in the womb, I wasn't alone." Tears start streaming down her cheeks.

I pull her close again. I press her against my chest and kiss the top of her head. "You're not alone. I'm here." Not for the first time, I wish I could take away some of Ali's pain, alleviate her fear, fill in some of the gaps in her life when she didn't feel loved.

She sobs against me, moistening my skin, and time ticks by. I know I should get to work, that someone or something will be waiting for my arrival, but I don't care, because nothing is more important right now than comforting Ali.

33

ALI

SEBASTIAN PACES AROUND THE ROOM. "Shouldn't he be back by now?"

"I don't know," I say for the umpteenth time. Hospitals make me nervous. I'd rather wait anywhere else. I wish Jill were here. I feel so trapped with only my brother in this hospital room. "I'm going to get some air."

"I'm going with you," he says.

"One of us should wait here in case he returns."

"He'll be asleep," Sebastian says matter-of-factly, not getting the hint.

We've been at the hospital since early this morning. This is the most time I've spent with my brother in decades. We're both agitated and ill at ease and it's not helping us to bond—to make up for all the time that we lost.

He follows me down the corridor and outside the hospital.

"Let's go where I can smoke."

"You don't smoke."

"I do today," he says.

I hope that's all he does. I watch him walk to the smoking area. This man who was once my little brother—our little brother. When it comes down to it, we're both equally screwed up, we just manifest it in different ways. And then I can't help but wonder if my sleeping with Jill is me acting out in some way—like Sebastian with the coke—or if it's real. It felt real yesterday, when she held me like that and I, for at least half a second, came to believe that what she predicted would come true. That Dad would be all right. Because now that he's in the operating room, this stoic, moody, dark man unconscious and utterly vulnerable, his life in the hands of his surgeon, it strikes me he's only human. Maybe what he did for us was the best he could do. It never felt like much, like there was never enough of his attention for the three of us, but maybe that was truly all he had to give after his wife died.

I join Sebastian and willingly stand in a cloud of smoke. He takes such light drags from his cigarette he may as well not be smoking at all. But I don't berate him for it. Because I feel exactly the same way he does.

"What if he doesn't make it," he suddenly says, "what happens then?"

"He's going to make it." I'm still Sebastian's older sister. It's still my job to comfort him. At least it is today.

He gives a terse nod then stubs out his half-smoked cigarette. We walk away from the hospital doors for a few minutes in silence, then, still in silent agreement, turn back. Being here together is all we can do. It's the best we can do for each other in this moment. We're not the type to sit crying while holding hands. We don't air our grievances, not even under pressure. We just live with them, day in and day out, and let them sit between us, except on some days, like today, when we automatically look past our differences for the simple reason that we're family. We grew up in the same house under the same circumstances. For others, that might provide endless topics of conversation, continued fodder for gossip and reminiscing, but for my brother and me it's more reason for silence.

The silence is more companionable than tense and that alone counts for a lot.

Later, when Dad is back in his room and still slipping in and out of consciousness, Sebastian goes out to get us some food. He could easily have something delivered, but now that the doctor has told us that the surgery went well and we don't have to sit with the fear of Dad dying any longer, I recognize Sebastian's desire to get away from the hospital for a little while.

I sit in the chair next to Dad's bed and close my eyes for a moment—I haven't gotten a lot of sleep the past few nights and the decompression is making my eyes fall shut.

"Ali," Dad whispers. "Ali."

"Dad?" I look up at him. "Are you okay?"

When he nods, his chin barely moves.

"Sebastian just went to pick up some food," I say, as though I have to make an excuse for my brother not being here—after all the times our father wasn't there when we needed him.

"Ali, in the recovery room," he whispers. "You dream of the weirdest things when you're coming out of the..."

"Anesthetic," I say.

"I dreamed I asked you if you wanted the company. Did I ever ask you that?"

"Dad, you shouldn't be talking so much. It's okay. I'm here."

"Ali, no, I need to know. Did I actually ask you—" He pauses to catch his breath. "Because in my dream, you said no. You didn't want to have anything to do with it."

"It was just a dream, Daddy. It's not real."

"It felt very real to me." He sags a little deeper into the pillow. "You should think..."

I can't make out what he says. I get up and look at him. I

should let him rest, but I'm too curious. "Sorry, Dad, I didn't get that."

"You should really think about it, Ali. I know what I sacrificed for that company." He suddenly reaches for my hand and curls his fingers around mine. "Don't make the same mistake I did, because, in the end, it's not worth it." He shakes his head. "I'm lucky and I know that's all I am, because you're here, by my side. That's just pure luck. It's not something I deserve, to have you here. It's—" His eyes flutter shut. His hand is still wrapped around mine, but his grip has softened.

His chest starts rising and falling in a steady rhythm. He's out again. Maybe I should leave the room when Sebastian comes back, to give him a moment like this with Dad. I shake it off as just a remnant of a dream he was processing. Because he did—sort of—ask me if I wanted to become CEO, although *ask* is perhaps not the best word for it. Even though it was formulated as a question, the answer was always already implied. Although, of course, I could have said no. But the thought never even crossed my mind. Not that becoming CEO of Lennox Breweries had ever been my goal—I always automatically assumed Sebastian would take over the company. But when you get asked, you say yes. Especially after Dad explained why Sebastian couldn't take over in the short term.

Is he having second thoughts?

The door opens and Sebastian walks back in with a Chipotle bag in his hands. He gives it to me.

"Has he been awake?" he asks.

"No," I reply. "Just in and out."

Sebastian has no reason not to trust me. But I can't tell him what Dad just said. Not only because they were just ramblings of a man waking up after surgery, but also because I need to think about it—and call Jill and tell her about it.

34

JILL

ALI CAME STRAIGHT OVER to my apartment from the hospital.

"It just made me think," she says. "Because it has thrown me." It's late and she looks tired. She's been by her father's bed all day.

"You should get some sleep. Proper sleep, I mean."

"Can I stay here?"

"Of course." I say it without thinking. I wouldn't dream of sending Ali home right now.

"It's just I hadn't expected a question like that to throw me so much. That's the real issue." She sounds like she's just rambling now, thinking out loud. I was hoping she'd let it go—because if Ali's having second thoughts about her future, that impacts my plans as well—but it doesn't look like she will. I can be a sounding board for her, but not much more than that. All of this is, of course, complicated by how I feel about her. But that, too, seems to be taking a back seat to what her father said when he was barely conscious.

"Then you should take some time to truly examine what you want."

She looks at me. She's leaning against the windowsill where

I undressed her last night. "Have you never wanted anything for yourself other than always work-work-work?"

Maybe this is another reason why I've become so comfortable as a single woman: being spared from too inquisitive questions.

"There have been times," I say, then stop, hoping that's enough for Ali.

"When?"

I walk over to her and lean against her. "Work has been good to me. I know that sounds like a massive cop-out, but it's what got me over my break-up, and then I started getting promoted, and along the way I found something I'm really good at and that I enjoy doing. And now… here I am."

"It doesn't sound like a cop-out." She shifts her weight and slants her body against mine. "I don't really know you that well, yet. I'm just curious."

"Surely, while you were away, you must have wondered about your future." I don't know Ali very well yet, either, but I'm keen to. "What did you see when you imagined yourself ten years down the line?"

"Honestly, I never saw myself becoming top dog at LB. Never. But I was open to it, instantly, when Dad suggested it."

"But what *did* you see?"

"Nothing. Because I always believed that picturing myself in the future was a luxury I couldn't afford." She scoffs. "I always knew I'd never have to worry about money. But… I don't know. Maybe finding someone who could love me."

"You're very easy to love," I say, without thinking again. "To like, I mean. You're very lovable. You know what I mean." I hope the burning in my cheeks hasn't translated into a high-pink blush, even though I know that it has. But it's quite dark in my apartment and Ali's looking straight ahead.

"So are you," she says, and puts her head on my shoulder. "What do you see when you think of your future?"

"I really don't know." I could tailor my answer to what Ali probably wants to hear, but it would only be a guess, and it would only be a half-truth. Telling her that I don't know is the closest to the truth I can come up with in this moment. I once made the mistake of envisioning a future for myself, in New York, with Melissa, until I learned what it felt like when the other person you're dreaming of a future with no longer holds you in her dreams at all.

"You don't dream?" Ali's voice has shrunk to a whisper.

"I live in the present," I say, sounding so very L.A.

"Because you're too busy to do anything else." She straightens, creating a small distance between us. She moves in front of me. "If you won't say it, Jill, I will. When I dream of my future right now, I see you in it."

"Oh, Ali." I shake my head.

"I mean it." She takes my hands.

"However tempting the thought… it's just not…"

"Then fuck the future," she says. "We only have the present. And today, we're together. Tomorrow, we'll be together. And the day after, and the day after." She smiles at me and it's a smile that's hard to resist, so I smile back, but not without trepidation making its presence known in the back of my head.

"What are you so afraid of?" she asks, when the moment has passed. "When you really think about it, what's there to be afraid of?"

"Your father," I say.

"My father is recovering from heart surgery. He's not the boss of LB anymore. And even if he was, what's the worst he can do?"

"Your father's respect is important to me. I've worked for him for a long time. He's taught me almost everything I know. He's been generous and—"

"What about me?" she asks. "Would you dump me to keep the respect of my father?"

"That's not something you can just come out and ask me, Ali. This is very complex."

She shakes her head. "It's really not. You're just making it complicated. Let me break it down for you." She steps away from me. "I like you." She throws in a grin. "A lot." A waggle of the eyebrows. "I get the feeling you like me too." She holds her palms up as if drawing a very simple conclusion. "Boom. That's it. We like each other, so we're together. And I don't know what the future will bring either, Jill. You may get sick of me tomorrow, or next week, or next month. And if that's the case, that's fine. But then at least we will have tried instead of running away from this."

"I think it's far more likely that you will get sick of me," I blurt out. "You're still so young. You have so many options. There are so many things you could do. So many people you could be with."

"But I want to be with you, Jill. Can't you see? Why can't you accept that?"

"Because… you're Ali Lennox. You're gorgeous and amazing and you turn heads whenever you walk into a room. You may not see it, but I do. Maybe you're used to it. I don't know. But me… I'm no match for you. And I'm far too old for you. What if you decide you want to have kids in a few years?"

"You're talking about kids now?" She puts her hands on her sides. "Jill… what you're basically saying is that you're scared. I'm scared, too. But it shouldn't stop us. Life's too fucking short for that."

It's something I can't argue about with Ali—of course, for her, life is short. But her experience is not mine. And it's bad enough that I've let her interrupt the quiet, hard-working life I've built for myself. And now, if I'm reading things correctly, she might not even want to work at LB anymore. "Maybe, in your world, everything's possible—"

"Stop saying things like 'in your world.' We live in the same world, Jill, you and I."

"From the very beginning, I've made it clear that I can't do this. That you're expecting too much of me."

"Have you ever stopped to wonder that perhaps you expect too little of yourself?" She takes a step closer again. "Sure, your work life is a big success. You're raking in the dough. You made it to COO. And there's no one else Dad trusts to be interim CEO. Open your eyes, Jill! You've seen what the stress has done to my father. At least he has two children to sit by his bedside. Who will you have when you're in the hospital?"

I know Ali's hurting and that she might be lashing out at the nearest person she can find, but she's also completely out of order. "My life choices are not something I need to defend, least of all to you."

"I don't want to fight with you." She holds up her hand.

"Then don't. Just stop it."

"Stop what? Stop talking? Or just stop… being with you?"

In her eyes, I see her scream for help. She came here because she's had an emotionally exhausting day, because she doesn't want to be alone tonight. She came to sleep in my arms, and I would have let her, I would have pulled her into a warm hug and told her everything would be okay, if only she'd just let me be me.

"Clearly, I'm not the person you want me to be—the person you want for you," I say.

"Hell no, Jill. Don't put this on me now. I want to be with you. You're the one blocking this. You're the one standing in your own fucking way."

"This isn't a conversation we should be having right now, Ali. You're tired. We're both emotional. Let's get some sleep."

"I really don't think so." She moves away from me again. "I'm not staying where I'm not wanted."

"Ali, you're upset." I grab her arm. "Let's calm down. Let's just have a drink and sit with each other a bit. No bold declarations and no visions of the future."

She shakes off my hand. "Just be in the present." She scoffs. "You know what, Jill? You're a coward. And I prefer not to hang out with cowards. Life's too short for that, too." The pain in her glance has been replaced with disappointment. It hits me like a slap in the face. But it's too late to snap out of anything now. Ali has grabbed her bag and she's by the door. And what would I say? Because she's right. I am a coward. For that reason, I have no choice but to let her go.

35

ALI

My first thought, when I get into my car, is to drive to Madison's, but she's on a location shoot in Canada. Then, strangely, my second thought is to go see my brother. Because he's family and we had a bit of a bonding moment earlier. But God knows what state he's in after today. I run through the list of people I could call, but most of them, I'm sure, will be at some party or another. It's Friday night in L.A. and I don't feel like partying at all. I would have if the only thing going on had been Jill and me breaking up before it has properly started. I'd go out and have a few and forget about her—because that's what I will have to do in the end. But I can't do that with my father in the hospital. It doesn't feel right. That's why I drove to Jill's in the first place. That felt like the right place for me tonight. By her side, her arms around me, her kind gaze on me. Turns out that was the wrong decision as well.

So I just drive back to where I came from. Official visiting hours are long over, but that's one of the perks of being a Lennox. We don't have to stick to the rules if we don't want to. The private hospital is used to people like us. So I walk in without being challenged.

I gently knock on my father's door.

"Yes," he says, his voice much more vigorous than earlier. It's not the voice of someone just woken from sleep. "It's not like I can stop you from coming in," he mumbles.

I push the door open and enter.

"Ali?" His eyes grow wide. "What are you doing here? What time is it?"

"It's late, but I wanted to see you." I wonder if he remembers anything at all from our earlier conversation.

"Everything all right?"

"Yeah," I lie. "How are you feeling?"

"I feel surprisingly good, actually. Except I'm not allowed to get out of this bed."

"It's for your own good."

"I'm awake," he says. "And alive. So I really can't complain."

"I guess not." I give him a smile, but it's forced, and it probably shows. "Can I get you anything? Some more water?"

"You know they have nurses here who take care of me." Something bordering on a grin appears on his face. "What's up, kiddo?"

Kiddo? I can't remember him ever calling me that.

"My dad's just had heart surgery."

"Tell him about it." Maybe this is what he's like when he's mellow. I'm not sure I've ever seen him like this before. "It's Friday night and you're here with me. Call me crazy, or maybe the anesthetic hasn't worn off yet, but something about that isn't right. Is your brother coming as well? Is this some sort of post-heart surgery intervention?"

"No, Daddy. Don't be silly."

"Hm. It would be nice, I guess. The three of us in this hospital room, drinking tepid water, because that's all I'm allowed to have. I haven't had a bite to eat since last night."

I sit in the chair where I spent most of the day.

He tries to push himself up, but he doesn't have the strength yet.

"Do you... remember any of the things you said earlier today?"

He arches up his eyebrows. "Wasn't I asleep most of the day?"

"In and out." I watch him as he shifts in the bed and I can't help but wonder, just for a split second, what it would be like to have Jill here with me. I can't really picture it. Her connection to my father stands in the way of everything. So, in the end, maybe she was right to reject me—to reject us.

"What did I say?" Dad asks when he seems to have found a comfortable position.

"You'd had a dream in which I told you I didn't want to be CEO."

"Huh," is all he says.

"And then you asked me to really think about what I wanted. If I really wanted to be CEO and make the sacrifices it entails. Because of the..." I suddenly feel self-conscious repeating his words to him—words he spoke when he wasn't fully aware of what he was saying. "The sacrifices you made."

"They weren't sacrifices," he says. "They were choices, Ali. I don't remember saying any of that, but I have been thinking about these things a lot lately. What with being faced with my mortality and not being in good enough shape to be in charge at LB. That's probably why I said them while I was still half under." He exhales deeply. "Turns out, I don't stand by all the choices I've made." He closes his eyes for an instant. "I'm sorry," he whispers, as his eyes flutter back open.

I can hardly believe it. I know that if I tell Sebastian about this, he won't believe me—I wouldn't if it was the other way around. Our father is not a man who apologizes. Because this is so unexpected, I don't know what to reply. Is this even an apology I can accept? It's a bit vague—what exactly is he apologizing for? And with the raw emotional state I'm in, I could actually do with a little more.

"You did what you—" I start to say.

"I mean it, Ali."

I scan his face, looking for signs that they replaced the man hiding behind it during the surgery.

"I'm sorry too, for going away," I say.

"You never have to say sorry for that. Not to me." He scoffs. "I taught you to run away. That's how I see it. And I should have known better. I should have been there for you and Sebastian… and Leah, after your mother died. I'm the father. I know I was a shitty one. I know I'm indirectly responsible for Sebastian's drug habit. But you… Look at you. You're perfect, Ali. My perfect girl. How did you turn out like that? I know that I had next to nothing to do with that."

"Dad, I'm… far from perfect."

"You even came home when I asked you to." Something glistens in his eye. Is that a tear? If he starts crying, I'll have to leave the room. I won't be able to deal with that display of emotion. "I don't want the business to screw up the life you have planned for yourself, kiddo. Fuck the board and fuck the shareholders. Really. Do what you want." With a surprisingly swift wave of his hand, he wipes away the tear that threatens to roll down his cheek. "What do you want? Do you know? In general, I mean. Before I asked you to come back. What was your plan?"

"I had no plan, Dad. I was glad when you called. I was ready for a new challenge."

"What about your personal life? Don't make the same mistakes I made, Ali. If you're going to run LB, don't have kids. If you want kids, don't run LB."

"That's a bit dramatic." I need to lighten the mood.

"I know you kids think you can have it all these days, but

I'm telling you, and I know this from decades of experience, you can't. You have to choose."

"I'm thirty-five, Dad. I'm single, and a lesbian. I won't be getting pregnant any time soon."

"Why are you single? A girl like you. Why aren't there women lining up in my hallway, asking for your hand? I know how Sebastian treats his women—another something to take responsibility for. The way I treated some of the women I met after your mother died..." He pauses. I'm beginning to think I should have recorded this for posterity—if there ever is any. Or just for myself. And for Sebastian. And for Dad. But he seems lucid. "You're young. You should be falling in love. You should be enjoying life."

I roll my eyes.

"I know I sound like a sentimental old fool, but..." he shakes his head once. "I'm glad you're here, Ali. Not just in L.A., but here, with me, tonight." He exhales deeply. "Will you do your old man a favor?"

"Sure."

"Tell me about your life. You're my daughter and I hardly know anything about you. I can always read about what Sebastian's been up to in the tabloids, but you..." He holds out his hand. I can only stare at it in disbelief. "I know so little of your life. And that's my fault. I want to know everything about you before I die."

"Jesus, Dad. You're not going to die any time soon." His hand hangs limply between us. Does he really want me to take it in mine?

"I might have, if you hadn't talked some sense into me." He shakes his head more forcefully this time. "It really made me see what kind of a stubborn old fool I can be." He wiggles his fingers about. "Come here. You don't have to tell me your entire life story at once. Just tell me one thing. Tell me about the last woman you fell in love with."

I scoff and shake my head. "Trust me, you don't want to know about that."

He grins at me. "I do. I very, very much do. Please, Ali, tell me."

Because he looks so pale and just out of surgery and is lying in a hospital bed, I at least take his hand. I let him wrap his fingers around mine, the way he did in his sleep this afternoon.

"There's someone," I say. "Someone I really, really like, but…"

"But what?" He squeezes my hand. "Give me one good reason why you can't be with this woman you really, really like?"

"Dad." I chuckle. "You really don't want to know."

"Come on. Indulge me. Just for five minutes, let me be the kind of father you confide in. The father I never knew how to be."

"It's you," I blurt out. "The reason is you."

"Me? This sick old man in a hospital bed? How do you figure that?" He smiles the kind of smile I've never seen on him before.

"I'm in love with Jill." I look away. Tears prick behind my eyes.

"*My* Jill? Jill Gold?" A silence falls. "Ali, look at me."

"No." I drop his hand and stand up. "This is ridiculous."

"Ali. Please."

I tower over his bed. I don't know why I told him. Maybe because, for half a minute, I wanted to have a parent I could tell things. Or maybe just to get a rise out of him. To punish him for what he's trying to do tonight—make up for a lifetime in five minutes.

"Does she feel the same way about you?" he asks.

"I don't know."

"I bet she does." He nods at the chair. "Will you sit back down?"

I glance at the chair as though it has become my biggest enemy.

"Or stand. It doesn't matter. But listen to me, please. Take it from a man who has squandered all the love he ever had at his disposal. I will not stand in your way. If you're in love with Jill, then be with her. Because you know what? Nothing else matters. It really fucking doesn't, Ali. And if you're afraid to be with her for some reason, then find a way to be unafraid, but don't use me as an excuse, because I refuse to be your excuse."

"It's not me who's afraid. It's her."

"Okay. Well. We'll see about that." He glances around. "Where's my phone?"

"Why do you need your phone?" His phone is hidden in a locker he doesn't have the code to yet.

"To text Jill to come and see me first thing in the morning."

"To tell her what?"

"To tell her that she has my blessing, damn it. You both do."

"Dad, seriously, what do they have you on? Is there morphine in that IV drip?"

"If you won't give me my phone, then give me yours." He ignores my question.

"I can text Jill myself, thank you very much."

"Do it now. I need to see you do it."

"Dad, you need to calm down. You're not supposed to be this agitated."

"I'm not agitated." He doesn't look particularly agitated. "All I want for you and Sebastian is to be happy. Despite having me as a lousy father. Despite losing your mother and your sister. It's all I want. I'd sell the brewery tomorrow if it meant securing your happiness. You probably don't believe me, but it's true."

"Why don't we see how you feel about that tomorrow?"

"Tomorrow doesn't matter, Ali. Every time I go to sleep now, I'm aware I might not wake up again. Which is why I'm telling you now. Be happy. Do what gives you joy. Be with Jill fucking Gold." He shakes his head. "Jill Gold," he repeats. "It is a surprise, though. I'm not sure I should be subjected to surprising announcements like that."

"You asked for it."

"I know. I know I did, Ali. I thought that perhaps you'd fallen for some D-list actress." He sniggers. "Not the woman who's been my second in command for years." He sighs. "I'd like to say I know her well. And you do get to know a person when you work closely with them day in and day out but, to tell you the truth, I don't know much about her personal life. I do know that she's whip smart, highly reliable, and one of the most loyal employees I've ever had."

"Are you really saying that you wouldn't mind if Jill and me… got involved?"

"Sounds to me like you're involved already." He holds out his hand again. "Phone."

"No."

"How else will you know if I'll still stand by this in the morning? I need to speak to her, anyway."

"I'll text her myself." Hands trembling, I dig my phone out of my bag.

36

JILL

When Ali texted me, at first, my heart lit up like the screen of my phone. But it was just a brief message to say that Jeffrey wanted to see me. In a way, I was glad it was just that. It's time to end this once and for all. It's time to face Jeffrey, to look him in the eye, and know, in my bones, that his daughter will mean less and less to me as time passes, as life goes on. When I look at him, I will be reminded to keep my work life and private life totally separate. And, this time, I will truly move on.

Now that I'm about to knock on his hospital room door, my palms are clammy, however. It's fucking with my head that I slept with his daughter—twice. But I'm about to see him in his pajamas a day after he had heart surgery.

"Jill." He's sitting up and looks quite chipper. "Thanks for coming."

"Of course." I put the fruit basket I brought for him on the windowsill. "How are you?"

"Something has come to my attention," he says, his voice still light and upbeat.

"I really don't think you should concern yourself with work right now. Your only focus should be getting better." I know

I'm saying it in vain. Telling Jeffrey not to think about work is like telling a toddler they can't go out and play. They'll just want to do it more.

"It's not about work, Jill." He fixes his gaze on me. It's the first time I notice that Ali has his eyes. "It's about my daughter."

Instantly, heat rushes to my cheeks. What about Ali?

"We had a frank chat last night. Extremely frank, in fact." Is that the beginning of a smile on his face? In that case, Ali must have assured him she'll want to follow in his footsteps at LB.

"Good." Or maybe he wants to end my very short reign as interim CEO already.

"I was prying into her personal life. Really prying, like an old aunt would do."

I swallow hard, but try to keep my face neutral. Surely, Ali didn't tell him about us.

"But I just wanted to know something about her. I know that she's an amazing woman and that I'm not the reason why she has become so remarkable. She's less self-destructive than Sebastian. And she carries herself so well, you know? When I look at her, I see someone who can really thrive. I can't help but feel a little bit of pride, even though I was never there. I didn't nurture any of the attributes that made her into who she is today. But she's so strong. So resilient. When she came to see me, out of the blue, last night, I couldn't believe my luck."

I'm hanging on every word Jeffrey's saying, even though I have no clue where he's going with this. I'm also not the best person to sing Ali's praises to today, but I can hardly stop him. And I agree with everything he says.

"Then, she told me that she met someone she really likes."

My heart leaps into my throat. Did Ali tell Jeffrey? What kind of conversation did they have last night? I can't picture it. Then again, there are many things about this family that I can't picture.

"And that *I* was the reason it isn't working out."

"Look, um, Jeffrey," I begin, even though I don't know what to say to him. This is my worst nightmare coming true. I don't want to have this conversation. Ali knows that—she must. Is that why she told him? Is this my moment of reckoning?

"I will not stand in the way of my daughter's happiness. I've done enough of that."

"W—what do you mean?"

"I told Ali last night and I'm telling you now: you have my blessing."

Christ. Ali could have let me know. Why didn't she? Maybe she didn't believe Jeffrey's blessing would make it through the night.

"If you want to be together, you should be together," he says.

I nod because I still don't know what to say. These are not the kind of conversations Jeffrey and I have.

"But... there is one caveat."

Of course there is. This is still Jeffrey Lennox I'm talking to.

"If you're going to be with Ali, I don't want you to be the COO of LB." He shakes his head. "Because I can't give my blessing to something I know is doomed."

"Excuse me?"

"I was never there for my family because I was always working, Jill. I don't want history repeating itself for Ali."

"Are you kidding me? You want me to resign?"

"If you're serious about her." He just shrugs, like he just asked me to take a day off instead of a massive step back.

"This is bullshit, Jeffrey, and you know it. How can you claim to give us your blessing and then ask me to quit? Then you might as well retract your words. I've given my life to LB. I haven't—"

"Or maybe you don't have to resign, Jill. Just take a step back. Because, yes, you're right, you've given your life to LB. So how can you make Ali happy if you continue to live only for your work?"

"That is not your call to make." I stand up and grip the bar at the end of his bed. Who is he to suddenly wish all this happiness on his daughter? I've probably spent more meaningful time with Ali in the past few weeks than he has in all of the thirty-five years of her life.

"Yet, I'm making it," he says.

"Oh, no, you're fucking not, Jeffrey. I'm not a pawn you can move from here to there. I'm not an ingredient you can disperse while, very belatedly, trying to make your daughter happy, or trying to redeem yourself as a father." I look into his gaunt face. He doesn't look so chipper anymore. "If Ali and I are going to be together, it will be on our terms and our terms alone. So, thank you for your rubbish blessing. And fuck you."

I grab my purse and make to leave.

"Jill, wait," he says. I can tell he's straining his voice. "Please."

"I'm leaving. You can apologize to me later. But let me tell you this: you're still a shitty father." I storm out of his room and bang the door shut. The sound reverberates through the quiet hospital corridors. I'm so angry, I have to steady myself against the wall. Who the hell does Jeffrey Lennox think he is?

I take a few deep breaths. I can see a nurse walking over to me and I don't want to be asked any questions. I smile at her as I walk out. What was Ali thinking? Then again, now he knows. And I have some thinking of my own to do. Because, clearly, things have changed. I'm just not sure yet if they have done so for the worse or the better.

Without thinking, I drive in the direction of Ali's house.

37

ALI

"A HEADS-UP WOULD HAVE BEEN NICE," Jill says, as I let her in. "I walk into Jeffrey's room and he gives me this speech about your happiness, after which he proceeds to tell me that he knows about us." She huffs out some air. "Fuck, Ali."

"I'm sorry. I didn't know what to think. Honestly, Jill. It's like I was talking to a different person last night."

"Oh, let me assure you that he's still very much the same."

"What do you mean?"

She inhales deeply. "I'm still getting over the fact that he knows. I didn't want him to know, Ali. I know that man. I know what he can be like. Already, it's made my position untenable."

"Hey, calm down." I gently nudge her into the living room. "What did he say?"

"You obviously had a heart-to-heart with him. And I'm glad that you did. He really does want you to be happy. So much so, that it has suddenly become his prime concern, but... he gave me an ultimatum. He told me, in no uncertain terms, that if I want to be with you, I can't be COO as well. That I would need to take a step back at LB."

"He said what?" My head hangs down for a second, then I look up at Jill. "I'm so sorry, Jill. What did you say?"

She pulls her lips into a half-smile. "I told him to shove his ultimatum up his ass." She bursts into a chuckle and I do the same.

"It's the only possible reply," I say. My chuckle transforms into a full-on belly laugh. "Fuck him." I can't believe my father would say that to Jill. Then again, should I really be so surprised?

"The funny thing is, though," Jill says, "that he made it sound as though his demands came purely out of the goodness of his own heart. He didn't spend enough time with you when you were a kid so now I somehow need to make up for that."

"I don't even really know what it feels like to have a parent worry about me like that." If my dad hadn't spoken to me the way he did last night, I'd find this all very hard to believe. "I'm sure he does worry about Sebastian and me, but never openly. As if that would be admitting a weakness."

"It is admitting to a weakness. Being a parent... we don't know what it's like, Ali. He does."

"I still can't believe he said that to you." I arch up my eyebrows. "Just like I can't believe the things he said to me last night."

"It's a lot. First the surgery. Then what happened between us yesterday. Now all this. I bet you didn't sign up for any of this when you decided to come back to L.A." Jill's kindness radiates in her smile.

"And now that he knows," I say. "Where does that leave us?"

She nods slowly, then glances at me. "I don't know."

"When you remove all the bullshit"—My heartbeat is doing a funny jump as I speak—"And only look at the essence of what we want, which is, if you don't mind me speaking for the both of us, to be together—" I stop. I really shouldn't be speaking for the both of us. "Do you want to be with me?"

"Ali," Jill says. "I do, but it's so complicated—"

"No, it's no longer complicated. The only complications are in your head." I stop myself again. Being too forceful with Jill has gotten me into trouble before. "Dad knows."

"Yeah, and he basically forced me to resign."

"I know that's what he said to you, but that's not what he said to me last night. He told me to be happy. He assured me that my and Sebastian's happiness are all he wants now. It's a little late, but still, I'm inclined to believe him. Either way, it doesn't matter. It's not about what my dad wants, anyway. It's about what we want. My father has no right to try to control us."

"We'll be working together and—"

"Jill, stop. Just stop making up reasons. Just tell me: do you want to be with me or not?"

She looks at me again, her glance careful at first, but then there's a small shift in the set of her jaw, the tension in her shoulders recedes, and her smile grows deliberate and a little wild. "Fuck, yeah." She walks toward me. "Yes, I want to be with you, Ali."

I take her hand and pull her closer. "About fucking time." I curl my arms around her and kiss her on the lips. "I'll talk to my dad. I'll set him straight."

"I believe I've already done that."

"Jill Gold." I give her an approving smile. "Perhaps the only person on the planet brave enough to stand up to Jeffrey Lennox."

"Well, he was in the hospital, looking quite frail despite the expensive pajamas."

"I suppose, in a way, he was defending my honor."

"Your honor?" She slants toward me and kisses me below the ear. "Last I checked, there wasn't much left of that."

"How dare you speak to me like that," I whisper in her ear. I'd like to say so many other things to her, but a quick quip is all I can manage, because Jill's lips are traveling the length of my neck and soon I won't be able to say anything anymore at all.

38

JILL

"I'M NOT SURE ABOUT THIS." I pull Ali away from the open door.

"Come on." She tugs my hand toward her. "United we stand and all that."

"The man just had bypass heart surgery. We should check with his doctor first." I know I'm making excuses. Standing up to Jeffrey, in the heat of the moment, was one thing, facing him alongside Ali is another thing altogether.

"Seeing us together is not going to give him a heart attack, okay?" She stands still in front of me. "If anything, it will make his old heart swell with happiness." She snorts. "That was too much."

"I just don't feel very comfortable."

"Neither do I, but we should just get it over with. Let's just talk to him. Show him this is real. And get on with our lives."

"But—"

"No." She tugs at my hand again. I wriggle myself free from her grasp, but she doesn't stop. She enters Jeffrey's room. My only other option is to leave the hospital—and let Ali deal with her father alone. I won't let her do that. So I follow her inside.

She's standing at the foot of his bed. Sebastian is sitting in a chair in the corner. *Great.*

"Well, look at that," Jeffrey groans. "Everyone's here. Shall we get Evelyn to come as well? She can take notes."

"Dad," Ali seems unperturbed by her brother's presence.

Sebastian just nods at me. He looks like he had a rough night.

"Hi Jeffrey," I say. "How's the old ticker?"

"Old is the right word for it," he says, and fixes his gaze on me. All the things he said yesterday come flooding back and I remember, most of all, that he still owes me an apology. Because it's not Ali and I who are in the wrong here. It's him. He shouldn't have tried to control me the way he did—it wasn't just infuriating; it was condescending.

My presence doesn't seem to surprise Sebastian at all, even though Jeffrey being in the hospital is a private affair. Or has Jeffrey told him? I glance at him from the corner of my eye. He doesn't look like a guy in the know. He looks like a boy trying to please his daddy by showing up, even though he'd much rather be sleeping off his hangover.

"Dad," Ali repeats. "Jill and I want to talk to you."

Jeffrey makes a dismissive gesture with his hand. "There's no need."

"Why do you and Jill want to talk to Dad?" Sebastian asks, his voice sounding as gruff as the stubble on his chin.

"It's private," Ali says.

"Is it about LB?" Sebastian asks.

"No." Ali's very curt with her brother.

"Then what's it about if Jill's involved?" He squints at me.

"I just told you that it's private. Can't you take a hint?"

"Ali," I say. "Why don't you talk to Sebastian outside for a minute. I'll talk to Jeffrey."

"But we were going to—"

I interrupt her. "It's fine. Just go. Tell him."

"Tell me what?" Sebastian's already gotten up. He looks at Jeffrey and, for a split second, I fear Jeffrey might just blurt it out.

"Fine," Ali says. "Seb, can I speak to you outside for a minute?"

Sebastian shrugs and follows her out of the room.

When it's just Jeffrey and me in the room, I give him time to speak—I wait for my apology.

"Don't hurt her," he finally says, after a few long minutes of silence. "Please, Jill, do anything in your power to keep her from getting hurt again."

I'm taken aback by his words because they're not what I had expected. I also never imagined speaking to Jeffrey about his daughter like this—with romantic intentions. On top of that, what he asks of me is not something I can promise.

"I think you can probably help with that." For the first time since setting foot in his room, I look Jeffrey in the eye. I'm looking into the eyes of an old man, someone quite possibly nearing the end of his life.

"Maybe," he says. "But Ali has always been her own woman. The absolute opposite of a daddy's girl." The shape of his lips resembles a smile, but the rest of his face doesn't cooperate with the sentiment. "Look, I know I'm being a fucking cliché here, what with reaching out to her while I'm in here. Almost like a death bed confessional." He scoffs. "But the truth is that I am now one of those fathers who wishes he could go back in time and be there for his children when they needed him the most. I wasn't strong for them. I hid my weakness behind my work. It was the perfect excuse. So giving you and Ali my blessing is the least I can do." He sounds so tired again all of a sudden, but I have to ask. I need to know.

"What about your ultimatum?"

locks his gaze on mine again. "I did with that as I was A glint in his eye. "By you." And that's all he has to say ut it. "When Sebastian arrived earlier, I half-expected him confess to me that he was sleeping with Anton."

I burst into a chuckle. "Nah, I really don't see that. Anton's way too uptight." Anton has been Lennox Breweries' Chief Financial Officer for years.

"I always thought *you* were uptight, Jill." Jeffrey's entire face is smiling now.

"Excuse me?" I can't continue my part in our banter—which is brand new in our relationship—because, from the hallway, noise flares up.

"Looks like it's not me you have to worry about," Jeffrey says. "I don't know what I'm going to do with Sebastian. Ali will land on her feet. But Seb… I don't know."

"Sebastian will be all right."

"Yeah." Jeffrey doesn't sound very convinced.

Then Ali and Sebastian waltz back into the room. Sebastian gives me a silent once-over, then shakes his head. I look at Ali, who rolls her eyes at me.

"I'm tripping," Sebastian says. "I swear I didn't take anything, yet I'm standing here, in my father's hospital room, tripping like it's nobody's business. Because my sister has just told me that she's fucking the COO of LB and that you…" He looks at Jeffrey. "Told her that is okay?"

It doesn't look like Sebastian will be all right any time soon.

"Seb," Jeffrey says. "You need some time to wrap your head around it. That's all."

"Oh, I don't. I know what's going on here. They'll be ganging up on me all the time—it'll be Ali and Leah all over again."

The unexpected mention of Leah's name fills the room with a sudden, brittle silence.

"What are you talking about?" Ali asks.

"Nothing. I just… I'm going to need some guarantees, that's all."

"Tell us what you mean, son," Jeffrey says. "About Leah."

Oh Christ. What have I gotten myself into? It's beginning to feel like family therapy.

"Ever since I can remember, Ali and Leah formed this front, this inseparable unit, that was always out to get me. I could never find a way in with them, no matter how hard I tried. And then Leah died, and of course Ali was shattered, but so was I. But once again, because it was always Ali and Leah, my grief didn't seem to matter as much. But I loved her too, okay? She was my sister, too." He looks like he has something else to say, then stops abruptly.

"I'm sorry, Seb. I never realized," Ali says. "I was always too caught up in my own shit."

"No kidding." Sebastian sits down.

"But Jill and me being together has nothing to do with Leah," Ali continues.

"I won't allow you to make me feel like an outsider in *our* family's company, Ali. Even when you become the big boss." His voice breaks a little.

And there we have it, I think. All Sebastian wants is to follow his father. It's been written all over his face since the first time he set foot in LB headquarters.

"Okay," Jeffrey says. "Thanks for… sharing." He reaches for the cup of water next to his bed. "Good meeting," he tries a joke, but his eyelids are droopy.

"Do you need help?" I ask. "A nurse?"

He shakes his head. "Just some rest, I believe," he says.

Ali, Sebastian, and I look at each other and, at least in that moment, we can find an understanding. We leave Jeffrey in peace and as we walk to the hospital's exit, I think it's very telling that Sebastian's most obvious concern about me being with his sister, is his position in the company.

"Do you want to hang out?" Ali asks, once we're outside.

"No. I need some time to think," Sebastian says, and skulks off.

39

ALI

"SEBASTIAN WAS RIGHT," I say, as I stare down at the headstone of Leah's grave. "It was always me and her against him. It really wasn't fair."

"You were kids," Jill says, shuffling her feet.

"Not all the time." I stand a little closer to her. "Thanks for coming with me."

"Of course."

"That got quite heated. Perhaps I should have known that Sebastian would be there." I look at the calligraphed letters of Leah's name, the dates underneath, bracketing her short life. "Sebastian can be such an asshole, but I'm no angel either."

Jill curves an arm around my shoulders and only because she pulls me close to her, only because she makes me feel safe—loved—do I even consider saying what I'm about to say. "A few weeks after Leah died, after the first shock had worn off, and the grief just slammed into me minute after minute, I wished... I wished it were Sebastian who had died in that car crash instead of Leah." I pull away from Jill a little. "It's dreadful to think about now. It's truly appalling, I know that. I'm so ashamed."

"You were grieving. You were just trying to hold on. And thoughts are just thoughts. Fleeting things that, most of the time, don't mean a whole damn lot."

"I've never told anyone that. Not even the grief counsellor I saw when I was living in London."

Jill tugs me toward her again. "You can tell me anything."

"So can you," I say.

Jill nods, then looks at me, as though she already has something to tell me. "Maybe... we should have a conversation with Sebastian. Maybe we shouldn't shut him out the way we've been doing."

"Really?"

"Give it some thought, Ali," she says. "He has his issues, but you only have one brother." She purses her lips—it makes them look so kissable again. "What Jeffrey said to me last night was completely out of order, because he has no right to make such demands of me, but, somewhere in there, he might have had a point."

"What are you saying?"

"I'm saying that plans can change, because circumstances change."

"You're going to have to be a little less cryptic. This is too important to be vague about."

"Remember when you asked me to go to Paris with you?"

"Of course. We were meant to be there right now." It seems like I asked Jill to hop on a last-minute plane with me weeks ago, whereas it's only been days.

"I would have gone with you. I might not have been able to admit it to myself, but I wanted nothing more than to go to Paris with you."

"We'll go soon enough."

"Maybe, or maybe not. Because we might be too busy." She narrows her eyes. "We both have a big financial and emotional stake in LB. But it doesn't mean we should devote our entire lives to it. There are other solutions."

"Such as?"

"Such as... I can delegate more, reduce my workload a bit. And instead of you being the future CEO, you and Sebastian could both be CEO. You could both be in charge. Sebastian would be happy—well, he may grumble about having to share, but that's his problem. He'd have the title and all that comes with it. He wouldn't need to spend his time and energy coveting it and undermining us while doing so. It would be a way to make amends with him, possibly the only way. And, more importantly, we would have more time to live our lives."

"Jesus, Jill. I think you may need to take me back to the hospital. I think I'm the one having a cardiac event." I smile to make sure she knows I'm joking.

"It's worth considering."

I huff out some air. "He'd need to get clean first. Properly clean."

"Of course. This doesn't have to happen tomorrow. You have a pretty capable interim CEO. No rush."

"She'll have to prove herself," I say. I press myself against Jill. Out of the corner of my eye, I see Leah's name—the shape of the letters long ago imprinted in my brain. I never thought I'd experience a moment like this standing next to my sister's grave, but here I am.

"I'm sure she'll do her best," Jill says, and kisses me gently on the cheek.

"I'll think about it. I promise."

"Talk to your dad about it while he's still in the hospital. It seems to mellow him."

"We should make a list of all the things to talk to him about while he's in there."

"You're young, Ali. Even though you've dealt with more than your fair share of death, you're in the absolute prime of your life. You radiate health. But for me, seeing Jeffrey like that, actually seeing with my own eyes, what a life of very limited love and affection and a hundred percent dedication to work has done to him. It has given me pause."

"I will never be like my dad." I curl my arms around her neck.

"Who would have thought," Jill says, "that you coming back would change everything. To tell you the truth, I thought you were going to be a massive pain in my ass, and nothing more than that."

"I was going to be your boss."

"You still are."

I shake my head. "No. It's impossible for me to be your boss. Maybe on paper, but not in spirit."

"We'll see."

"We will." I kiss her, and, as I do, I no longer have eyes for Leah's gravestone.

Epilogue - Jill

40

JILL

Three Years Later

"How's your French?" I ask Ali.

"Très bon." She lifts up her glass of champagne. "Although I guess you'll have to take my word for it." She smiles before she takes a sip. She still looks very much like the woman who barged into my life three years ago, yet so much about her has changed as well. Her hair is short now—even shorter than mine—and she's wearing glasses. Once she and Sebastian took over from me as co-CEOs of Lennox Breweries, and she started attending public events in that function, I would glance at her from the corner of my eye and could hardly believe the transformation. As though, when you're a Lennox, being given a title will do that to you.

"I won't have to take your word for it." In the lead-up to our long-awaited trip to Paris, which is only the starting point of a two-month-long jaunt through France, I've taken French lessons. *"Monsieur,"* I say to a member of the cabin crew walking past my seat. "Can you tell me what time it is in Paris right now, please?" I ask him in French. It sounded better in my head, but then again, languages have never been my strong suit, and a couple of lessons can only teach me so much.

"Paris a neuf heures d'avance sur nous," he says. *"Donc il est huit heures du soir."* He finishes off with a wide grin, then leaves.

"Did you get that?" I ask.

"Of course," Ali says. "Did you?"

"It's 8 p.m. in Paris." I extend my arm over the table that divides the space between us. "But truth be told, I could do with some extreme immersion."

Ali takes my hand. "You can immerse yourself all you want for the next two months, babe," she says.

I nod. "How are you feeling?" It's been quite the experience to see Ali evolve from someone who regularly arrived at the office late, her lackluster attitude always on display, to the big boss who often stays long after I've gone home for the day. "Withdrawal's not too bad?"

"My phone's off," she says. "And I trust Seb."

"So do I." When we approached Sebastian about becoming CEO alongside Ali, it was like a switch flipped inside his head. As though that exact opportunity was what he'd been waiting for to fully get his act together. One of the reasons we're only going away for two months is because he's getting married to a woman he met during his last stint in rehab. The main reason, though, is that neither Ali nor I can imagine being away from Lennox Breweries much longer than that. And that way, Sebastian can go on his honeymoon without having to worry about the company too much.

I hold up my half-empty glass of champagne, which is promptly refilled by the same member of the cabin crew I just practiced my French with. I only wanted to make another small toast, but I accept his spontaneous top-up by emitting a few more sentences in broken French.

"To Paris," I say. "I thought we'd never make it."

"But we did." Ali narrows her eyes and leans over the partition. "My cougar and me."

I close my eyes and shake my head. "I asked you a million times, Ali. Don't call me that. I'm hardly a predator. If anything, you came after—"

"Just a joke." She leans all the way over and kisses me on the cheek. "Time for the COO to relax and expand her sense of humor."

"If I didn't have a sense of humor," I remind Ali, "we wouldn't be on this plane right now."

"What are you saying? That being with me is all a joke to you? Well, the past three years have been funny sometimes, but fuck, you worked me hard."

"I hope I did some other things as well." The past three years haven't always been a walk in the park, but we're here now, still together, finally on our way to Paris. While we set up the new structures at the company, and got used to our new roles, we always clung to the idea of one day going on that trip to Paris.

"One day, we'll have Paris," we used to joke, because that day always seemed so far away. But time did what it always does: it passed. It brought us here. And we're not quite in Paris yet, but we'll be there in a few hours, and I'm convinced that I'm much better off going now than when Ali first asked me three years ago, on a whim.

Because this is no longer a whim. Ali and I are in a long-term relationship that has been approved by both our families. Two nights ago, as a farewell, we had dinner at Jeffrey's house in Beverly Hills, with Sebastian and his bride-to-be. Jeffrey will never run the company again, although he will always find ways to meddle and have his say, but his heart has held up, and he's doing as well as can be expected.

Ali and I may tell ourselves we didn't need anyone's

approval, and maybe our love would have survived that particular hardship, but we did get Jeffrey's and Sebastian's blessing, avoiding a lot of stress. Sometimes, I think that it was mainly me who needed the Lennox blessing, because I'm the older one and, perhaps, I should have known better than to fall for Ali; but Ali, too, has flourished, slowly but surely, by tightening the ties with her family.

In order to do so, she had to go away, because that's how it is sometimes. Sometimes, the pain in one place can be too overwhelming to deal with, as though it accumulates because of the proximity of the people suffering, and it's only air and space and time that can make the worst of it evaporate, can make you breathe again. And Ali can breathe again now. She can thrive. And I do the same alongside her. It would be impossible not to.

ABOUT THE AUTHOR

Harper Bliss is a best-selling lesbian romance author. Among her most-loved books are the highly dramatic French Kissing and the often thought-provoking Pink Bean series.

Harper lived in Hong Kong for 7 years, travelled the world for a bit, and has now settled in Brussels (Belgium) with her wife and photogenic cat, Dolly Purrton.

Together with her wife, she hosts a weekly podcast called Harper Bliss & Her Mrs.

Harper loves hearing from readers and you can reach her at the email address below.

www.harperbliss.com
harper@harperbliss.com